RONNY COHEN

by Alexsandra Kyle

Order this book online at www.trafford.com
or email orders@trafford.com

Most Trafford titles are also available at major online book retailers.

Note for Librarians: A cataloguing record for this book is available from Library
and Archives Canada at www.collectionscanada.ca/amicus/index-e.html

Printed in Victoria, BC, Canada.

ISBN: 978-1-4269-1437-9 (sc)

*Our mission is to efficiently provide the world's finest, most comprehensive book publishing
service, enabling every author to experience success. To find out how to publish your book, your
way, and have it available worldwide, visit us online at www.trafford.com*

Trafford rev. 6/24/2009

 www.trafford.com

North America & international
toll-free: 1 888 232 4444 (USA & Canada)
phone: 250 383 6864 ♦ fax: 812 355 4082

To my darling Matt,
In hopes that you, too,
Will find your Kurt
Some day.

In memory of Harvey Milk,
And the continuation of his dream.
And that perhaps
One day
Intolerance
Of all kinds
Will be eradicated.

Chapter One

RONNY COHEN STEPPED out of his father's car and onto the scraggly lawn of his new high school. He took a deep breath and marveled at how different suburban air was from urban air. Although he lived for the city and loved being jostled through crowds, loved being surrounded by people, the suburban setting of his new school had its pros, too—namely the unpolluted air. He turned to wave to his father, but the moment the door had closed, Ronald Sr. had driven off. Ronny sighed. He was used to his father's harsh treatment, but he just wished that for *one day…*

A bell sounded in the distance, shaking Ronny from his thoughts. He hurried across the lawn, afraid that he would miss his second first day of public school.

Ronny had attended public school with his younger brother until he was fourteen years old. However, when Ronny had begun to doubt his sexual preference, his parents took it upon themselves to "cure" their son—by throwing him into a private boarding school. At first, he didn't mind (although the school was Catholic based, the other students were far from Catholic minded) but when his parents found out about the wild parties, many of which were hosted in Ronny's room, it was back to public school for Ronny Cohen.

Now, seventeen years old, Ronny Cohen was starting his senior year at Dickson County High School. It felt strange to be surrounded by so many students and not to know a single person.

He looked for his brother among the sea of faces as he headed to his classroom. His brother had insisted on taking the bus, not wanting to be seen with his older brother. Even so, Ronny wanted a comforting smile, if only for a moment.

He never did see his brother that morning.

About halfway through the day, Ronny finally noticed the heads turning in his direction, the eyes following him in the hallways. At first he couldn't figure it out, couldn't place why he attracted so much attention.

For a while, he thought it was his hair, until he saw some of the other haircuts around the school. Sure, his blond hair was streaked with charcoal grey highlights, but how did that compare to the girl with the rainbow hair? And his hair might be shorter in the back and longer in the front, but how did that compare to three-foot-high Mohawks? And were bangs really that ridiculous?

Then he thought maybe it was his bag. Not many guys at this high school had messenger bags to put their books in, but Ronny found it both comfortable and convenient—any high schooler's necessity.

During math, he wondered if it was his pants. The other guys wore jeans so loose and baggy that the waistband was practically at the knees. Okay, so what if his boxers *weren't* showing? How did that make him different? It just meant that he was *tasteful* instead of *disgusting*.

His shirt, maybe? Okay, so, he could have gone with a shirt that wasn't so form-fitting, but this was his favorite shirt. Or, maybe it was the gold glitter print…but it was advertising his favorite band! If the gothic kids could wear a nasty clown that hadn't been to the dentist in years in support of a heavy death metal band, he could support his favorite indie band. At least you could *understand* the lyrics of indie music, as opposed to having your eardrums raped by the insufferable screaming of heavy metal.

Or maybe it was his shoes. They were rather…blue. Electric blue, to be exact.

Or maybe it was the shark's tooth necklace that swung hypnotically around his neck when he leaned over to put his books in his bag. The necklace had been given to him by his friend Steven, and he never went a day without wearing it.

It wasn't until he was sitting alone at lunch that he realized it was probably a combination of those things. What he thought of as tasteful, other kids thought of as weird. What he thought of as grungy and disgusting, they

thought of as cool. He realized that in the atmosphere he was in, his attire totally screamed "gay."

He huffed in annoyance. He hated labels, and he *especially* hated to be defined by his sexual preference alone. Well, he wasn't going to change his sense of style just because these other shmucks thought "grunge" was the new "hygienic."

Sitting in the lunch room, Kurt Vaughn contemplated how long he could hold his breath without passing out. Sure, Mitchell and Keith were his friends, but in his opinion, marijuana smelled awfully close to cat piss. He swung his legs around so he was sitting backward on the bench. Their idiotic slurs still reached his ears, and he wished he had remembered to grab his iPod before he had left that morning. Mitchell and Keith had been a lot cooler back when they were in elementary school, before they discovered drugs and alcohol.

Kurt glanced around the cafeteria, looking for some other friends he could hang out with for a while. His eyes fell on a blond boy sitting all by himself. Kurt recognized the boy from his math class but couldn't remember his name. Standing up suddenly, he decided to be friends with the new kid. He glanced back halfway across the cafeteria and realized that Mitchell and Keith hadn't even noticed him leave.

Dickson County High School, just like any other high school, had a long list of unspoken rules. First and foremost: Dress and act like everyone else if you want to have friends. Conformity was a big deal at their school. Even the nonconformists were conforming to nonconformity. This rule was the main reason why new kids usually didn't have friends their first day at Dickson, because they were just too different.

Kurt decided blatantly to ignore this rule. He wasn't big on following rules anyway. As he drew closer to the new kid, he wondered why this boy was ostracized by the other students. Sure, he seemed a little too…clean for the rest of the school, but was that really a bad thing?

"Yo," greeted Kurt when he was right next to the boy. "I'm Kurt Vaughn. We're in the same math class. Is there, uh, anyone sitting here?"

The boy shook his head, his soft blond hair brushing across his yellow-green eyes. He took a bite of his sandwich and stared silently at Kurt.

Kurt slowly sat down in the booth across from the silent boy. "I, uh, really like your shoes. They're my favorite color."

The boy smiled. "Thanks!"

Another heavy moment of silence settled over them. Kurt cast around for a new topic that might last more than two seconds. "So…you new around here?"

The boy grinned. "Well, yes and no, actually. I've lived in this city all my life, but I've been going to a private school since seventh grade. But, you might know my brother, Benjamin Cohen."

Kurt laughed. "Little Benji Cohen is your bro? Man, you guys look **nothing** alike! I **never** would have guessed you two were related!"

"I get that a lot."

The bell rang.

Kurt stood up and said, "Look, I'll see you around… Uh, I never did catch your name."

"Ronny. Ronny Cohen."

Kurt smiled. "All right. Well, see you around, Ronny."

Ronny watched Kurt walk out of the lunchroom before throwing his trash away. His heart was fluttering rapidly, and not just because Kurt had the body of a model. He was really happy that he had made a friend, even if it had only been for about five minutes. And those eyes…

Ronny walked into his lit class and stopped suddenly. There, sitting with his legs dangling over the edge of the desk with his head buried in a book, sat Kurt Vaughn. The fluttering came back tenfold, and Ronny felt a light red color come to his cheeks.

Kurt glanced up from his novel and smiled and waved at Ronny. He beckoned for him to come over as he closed his book. "Hey, Ronny. You can sit by me."

"Thanks…Kurt."

The bell rang, and Kurt slid off the desk and into his seat.

Because Kurt sat between himself and the teacher, Ronny spent a good portion of the class staring at his new crush instead of paying attention to the teacher and the boring lecture. They were going over subject-verb agreement, something that had been hammered into Ronny's head since he was a freshman.

Kurt Vaughn had dark brown hair that came just above his shoulders… or it would, if he would take out that hideous orange rubber band. Unlike the rest of the male population at Dickson County High, Kurt's blue jeans were his size and didn't fall haphazardly below his ass. He wore a bright yellow shirt with an orange lion with brown stripes. On the back, it said, "Support the ligers." He wore orange Converses to "match" his shirt.

Kurt turned around to face Ronny, his blue-grey eyes locking with Ronny's yellow-green ones. Ronny felt heat rushing to his cheeks. He felt like a kid who had just been caught with his hand in a cookie jar.

"Hey," said Kurt softly, "do you have your books yet?"

Ronny shook his head. "No, I pick them up this afternoon."

"Oh… Well, do you want to share my book?"

"Um, yes, please. Thank you."

Ronny's heart pounded in his chest, trying to break free from its rib cage prison, as Kurt scooted his desk closer. For a moment, Kurt's leg brushed against his, and Ronny felt light headed.

Oh, get a hold of yourself, Ronny scolded. *You've been around plenty of beautiful people before. Why is this one any different?*

Oh, but, *damn*, was he beautiful…

"Hey, Ronny, you all right?"

Ronny shook his head, wholly embarrassed. This crush needed to stop before it escalated too far.

"Uh, yeah, I'm fine. Thanks for asking, though."

"Hey, no problem. Any time, man."

Ronny Cohen was about to experience the horrors of a high school gym class.

He turned a pale shade of green when he opened the door to the locker room. Not only did it smell of three-month-old dirty underwear and rotting fish, but there were no air conditioning units in the gym locker rooms. The moment Ronny Cohen stepped into that locker room, he could feel sweat dribbling down his forehead. "Hot as hell" had taken on a whole new meaning.

Ronny weaved between the clusters of half-naked men until he reached his locker near the back of the room. He would much rather have been up near the door, so as to be able to get in and out as quickly as possible, but the locker was assigned to him. He would just have to suck it up and hold his breath that much longer.

Ronny glanced to his left as he pulled his shirt over his head and did a double-take. For his brother not to have shown his face all day, he was apparently quite a character to miss. Ronny almost didn't recognize little Benny Wenny, seeing as how he was surrounded by practically thirty of his friends, all laughing and cracking jokes about whatever tickled a freshman's fancy these days.

Deciding to embarrass Benny Wenny later by announcing their relation, he went back to changing. As he was pulling on his sneakers, however, he glanced up and noticed another familiar face…and right at that moment, Kurt Vaughn also decided to look around the locker room. Their eyes met, and Ronny offered a small wave and a smile. Kurt waved back before pulling off his shirt.

Ronny froze, his eyes glued to Kurt's torso. Not only could one iron a shirt on those rock-solid abs, but there was a large tattoo of a dragon along his back. The head of the dragon came over his right shoulder and breathed fire across his left breast. The tail of the dragon wrapped around front from his left hip, the tip of the tail curling around his navel. A shirt came over Kurt's head, and the beast was tucked away out of sight.

When Ronny stepped out of the locker room, he felt dizzy. He tried to blame it on the extreme heat of the tiny room…and that it had nothing to do with that—

Oh God.

Kurt waved Ronny over to stand with him.

"Hey, man, what's up?" Kurt said when Ronny finally stumbled over to him. "Okay, gym class is a little confusing at first, all right? First we stand against this wall until the coach finishes jacking off and comes out of his office… Then, he'll take roll, tell us to run for thirty minutes, and then we can take the rest of the time off or play basketball or something."

Ronny laughed. "How is that confusing?"

Kurt shrugged. "Trust me. It gets a little crazy sometimes. You have to stand at the right wall, run for a certain amount of time before you can walk… I don't know." Kurt flashed Ronny a grin, and Ronny felt himself getting swept away. "Hey, question: Did you have gym at your old school?"

Ronny shook his head and said, "No. Well, sort of. Once a week, we went outside to run a few laps or play sports and shit, but nothing big…"

Kurt stared at him for a few moments. "Hey, Ronny, your mouth is too pretty to use for cursing."

Ronny felt his cheeks redden. Did Kurt just call his **mouth** pretty? While Ronny was about to faint with happiness, Kurt barely seemed to notice the effect he had on the blond. Luckily, right at that moment, the coach started checking roll. Ronny took one glance at the 40-year-old man and felt his hormonal high come crashing back to the ground.

"All right, girlies!" yelled the coach. "Run for the next thirty minutes! Then go play some basketball and get that lard off your ass!"

Kurt grabbed Ronny's hand and took off running. Ronny felt a tingling sensation start in his wrist and shoot up through his body, turning his legs to jelly, and he found it rather difficult to keep up with Kurt's quick pace. He focused on an image of the coach and found running to be easier, the tingling in his body gone.

After a few minutes of all-out sprinting, Kurt finally slowed down. He didn't even register that he still had his hand clasped around Ronny's wrist as he said, "Hey, sorry for taking off like that, man. I just like running."

Ronny nodded before answering, "Nah, it's fine, but…are you on the track team? Because, damn, that was really fast!"

Kurt laughed. "No, I was never on track, but I used to be on the baseball team…until my best friend was caught with marijuana, that jackass. But, just because I knew him, I was ostracized. So I said, 'To hell with this! I'm not playing anymore!' And I quit. I mean, baseball relies on teamwork, and if they wouldn't work with me, well, what can you do?" He squeezed Ronny's wrist. "So, what about you? You do any sports?"

Ronny laughed bitterly. "Not since I went to St. Paul's Private Boarding School, where having teams and the concept of winning and losing is considered a sin."

"You hated it there?" Kurt's response was balancing precariously between a question and a point-blank statement.

"Hate?" Ronny repeated the word, letting all of the nuances flow through his body before answering. "Hate is too strong of a word. Let's just say, I disagreed with their principles—the headmaster's principles, I mean. The school itself was great, it's just… It's hard, you know?"

Kurt shook his head. "No, sorry, I wouldn't know."

Ronny smiled. Kurt had the attitude of being somewhat stupid, yet Ronny could feel the meaning and wisdom behind that statement. Instead of asking all the questions, Kurt was guiding Ronny and letting him keep control of the conversation.

"It's like this," said Ronny. He pulled on Kurt's wrist until they had slowed down to a walk. "Suppose there's something that you really believe in, that you really, truly believe in, but your idea is not accepted in most of society."

Kurt looked at him curiously. "What, like anarchy?"

"Yeah, sure, anarchy." Ronny flashed him a grin, letting him know without out-right saying it that he was most definitely not talking about anarchy. "Say you live in secret all your life, and no one knows you believe in this one idea. And then, one day, someone finds out. Now, you'd expect complete strangers to turn on you, but what you *don't* expect is for your family and your closest friends to turn on you as well. You would think that people would still view me as 'Ronny Cohen' with a bumper sticker attached that says 'Anarchist.' Instead, I'm ostracized. I'm viewed as an entirely different person."

"Damn, that must be hard," said Kurt quietly.

Ronny shrugged. "You get used to it."

Kurt looked angry. "What? No! You shouldn't 'get used to it!' No one should be treating you like scum in the first place!"

Ronny offered Kurt a small smile. "Hey, thanks for caring so much, but seriously, it's not a big deal—"

Kurt was livid now. "*Not a big deal*?" he shrieked. Ronny saw other students turn to look at them curiously, but Kurt paid little to no attention to the others. "Listen, Ronny, I've known you for less than a day, and I can tell you that no matter what ideas and theories about life you have, it doesn't make you a bad person! *They're* the ones that are bad! The people who would mistreat others just because it clashes with what they believe! We're not Crusaders! We're not jihadists!"

"Girls!" shouted the coach from across the gym floor. "If you don't get your asses moving, I'll come over there and *make* you move!"

Kurt rolled his eyes and pulled on Ronny's wrist until they were running again. As they passed the coach, Kurt called out, "Geez, Coach Jamey! Didn't you see us sprinting at the start of the class? Isn't that a free pass out of running for the last five minutes?"

The coach narrowed his eyes at Kurt. "No! Now keep that ass moving, Vaughn!"

"Yeah, yeah, whatever…" Once they had passed the coach, Kurt turned his gaze on Ronny. "So, Ronny Cohen, what is this big idea of yours that's gotten yourself pushed out of society, if you don't mind my asking?"

Ronny grinned and pulled his wrist free from Kurt's grasp. "I'll race you."

Kurt returned the grin and began sprinting, shouting over his shoulder, "You'll never beat me, not in a million years!"

Ronny remained directly behind Kurt until about five seconds before their running time was over. He used his last burst of energy to run at full-speed, successfully passing Kurt. The coach blew his whistle, and the two boys fell panting and laughing against each other.

Chapter Two

RONNY COHEN WOKE up a bit more eagerly for his second day of school than he had for his first. Even his foul-tempered brother didn't seem as bitter and maleficent.

He glanced down at his outfit with a smug smile, turning around and around in front of his full-length mirror. His green plaid button-up shirt made his eyes stand out just that much more. His khaki cargo pants hung loosely around his legs but accentuated his ass perfectly. His black shoes barely peeked out from underneath his pants, as if they were playing hide-and-go-seek with the world. He slipped his shark's tooth necklace around his neck and headed downstairs.

His parents, brother, and younger sister, Georgina, were already downstairs. His mother was by the stove frying eggs for herself and her husband, who was sitting at the table reading the paper and drinking coffee. Benjamin and Georgina were already halfway done with their bowls of cereal, both needing to catch the bus in a couple minutes. There was an unspoken agreement in the family that Ronny was not allowed to drive his siblings to school.

Georgina looked up from her cereal and smiled at her brother. She and Ronny were the only ones in their family with blond hair and yellow-green eyes. For being in seventh grade, she looked a lot more mature than she really was, and people often asked if she and Ronny were twins. Out of everyone in their immediate and extended family, she was the only one who accepted Ronny for who he was.

Georgina immediately noticed the spring in Ronny's step and, forgetting for a moment, decided to tease her older brother. "Little Ronny Cohen! You seem happy this morning, almost as if you're in lo—"

She stopped half-way through the word "love" and threw her hands up to cover her mouth. Her eyes, just barely visible above her hands, shone with fear.

Their mother dropped a raw egg on the floor, and their father nearly let his coffee cup slip through his fingers. Mrs. Margaret Cohen spun around to face her daughter. "*What* did you say?" she snarled.

Georgina did not dare remove her hands from her mouth and shook her head violently.

"*Remember* what we talked about, Georgina," she hissed, "about your brother and his—his *fantasies!*"

Ronny let his mother's harsh words roll off him like water on a duck's back. He poured himself a bowl of cereal and sat down at the table between Georgina and his father. Georgina waited until the others weren't watching before she mouthed, "I'm sorry," to her brother. Ronny smiled and squeezed her hand under the table. "I know," he mouthed back to her.

Ronny pulled up to the school and drove around for a few minutes before finally finding an empty spot in the student parking lot. For being ostracized, he sure did have a sweet ride, although it was all due to his eccentric uncle leaving it to him in his will. He grinned as he heard cat-calls following his cherry red convertible.

He climbed out of his car and happened to glance up just as Kurt was passing by in his blue pick-up truck. Kurt was already in the process of slowing down to admire the car when he saw it was Ronny's. He rolled down his window and called out, "Damn! Sweet ride, man!"

Ronny laughed. "Thanks, Kurt!"

"Hey, don't move from that spot! I'm going to park my car and be right over!"

"Sure thing."

Ronny felt giddy from the time Kurt came back all the way until they parted for first period. Even the glare his younger brother sent him as they passed in the hallway didn't dampen his mood.

It wasn't until right before lunch that Benjamin Cohen deemed it fitting to talk to his older brother. He pulled Ronny aside where no one would see them and hissed, "I'm going to tell Mom and Dad about your new little *boyfriend* if you don't quit hanging all over him."

"I am *not* hanging all over him!" Ronny retorted.

"Oh bull *shit*," Ben shot back. "You're practically *drooling* on him. I'm surprised you two haven't gotten a room."

"What the hell, Ben? Being gay isn't a *disease*! Stop making such a big deal out of this! Besides, what are Mom and Dad going to do? Make me transfer schools? *Again*?"

If looks could kill, Ronny Cohen knew he would be dead right now.

To make matters worse, Kurt chose that moment to show up. "Hey, Ronny! Hey, Benji! I was *wondering* when you two would talk to each other!"

With a terse, "Good morning, Kurt," Ben spun on his heel and walked angrily away.

Ronny blushed. "Uh, Ben and I don't really get along very well," he explained.

"He's against your ideas, too?" Once again, Kurt's reply tottered precariously between a statement and a question.

"Yeah, he is. He's most definitely against it…"

"I'm sorry to hear that." He surprised Ronny by grabbing onto his wrist and pulling. "Come on, let's go get some lunch!"

After getting his food, Kurt stopped by his table to apologize to Mitchell and Keith. "Hey, sorry, guys, but I'm going to sit with my friend Ronny today. Is that all right with you?"

Mitchell and Keith showed the emotion of a rock, and Kurt realized they were stoned.

"Right…"

Kurt took his tray and sat at the table with Ronny. He glanced from his cafeteria food to Ronny's lunch from home and back again. "Hey… You want to trade?"

Ronny wrinkled his nose at the hamburger. Even though the cafeteria food probably wouldn't taste half-bad, he had been spoiled with boarding school food. "Sorry, no can do, Kurt. I'm a vegan."

Kurt laughed. "You're not a vegan! You're eating a turkey sandwich!"

Ronny smiled.

For the most part, Ronny ate his lunch in silence while Kurt ran his mouth about the most random things. He started out by telling his life story before switching off and talking about dinosaurs, then roller coasters, then whales…

"Sorry, Ronny," said Kurt suddenly around a mouthful of French fries. "You must be bored to tears by now."

"Surprisingly, no," said Ronny with a wink. "It's nice to have someone to talk to."

"Someone who won't judge you?" Kurt noticed Ronny's look and quickly added, "I'm sorry, I'll stop talking about...about that idea of yours. Your anarchy."

Ronny offered a weak smile. "No, that's all right, it doesn't matter. I'll tell you about it one of these days, probably. Just...not right now."

"Yeah, but still, I'm sorry. I know it's an uncomfortable topic for you, yet I keep bringing it up." A strange look passed over his face. "I've got it! Okay, I've been embarrassing you. How about this: *You* ask *me* something embarrassing!"

Ronny laughed. At a quick glance, the idea was so stupid and childish, but the meaning underneath... It was really touching. Ronny paused, pretending to be thinking, but he knew exactly what he wanted to ask. "All right, Kurt... An embarrassing question... Hmm... How about...when did you get that tattoo?"

Kurt grinned. "That's not an embarrassing question! I would have told you about it anyway!" He pulled up his shirt to show off the tail curling around his belly button. "I got it for my sixteenth birthday. Sweet, right?"

"It's fucking *hot*!" The words were out of his mouth before he could stop them.

The look Kurt gave him made his stomach turn. For a second, he thought he was about to lose a friend he had only had for two days. "You don't curse very often, do you?"

Kurt's question confused him. "Well, no... I mean, they'd get super pissed at us for cursing at St. Paul's..."

"I told you yesterday: Your mouth is too pretty to use it for silly things like cursing." Kurt glanced at the clock. "Hey, come on, the bell's about to ring. Here, I'll throw away your trash for you."

Ronny had no idea how to react to Kurt. Was he flirting with him on purpose, or was that just his personality? Kurt obviously knew Ben (apparently "Benji" had quickly become the most popular kid in his grade), so had he heard stories about Ben's gay older brother? Was Kurt just messing with him?

Ronny told himself to calm down. Of course Ben wouldn't have told anyone he was gay. He had spent half his life denying that they were even *related*. It just must be Kurt's personality...

They walked together to their lit class. Ronny wasted another class period simply staring at Kurt, only bothering to pay attention when the teacher asked him a question.

The rest of the day flew by, and it was last period—gym. Ronny grimaced as he pushed his way through the half-naked boys to his locker in the back. Perhaps it wouldn't have been so bad, but the locker room smelled worse than a dead skunk.

At his locker, he found that if he turned just slightly, he could watch Kurt pull his shirt over his head…watch the dragon tattoo quickly disappear from sight as a new shirt came to cover it. Ronny blushed and quickly turned back around as Kurt reached to pull off his pants. Just because he had a crush on him didn't mean that he had to turn into a creepy voyeuristic pervert.

He pulled on his shoes and heard his brother sit on the bench beside him.

"Bet you like it in here, don't you, you sick freak?"

Ronny didn't answer. As accustomed as he was to his brother's constant taunts, they still stung. His own brother…

"I bet you like to look at all of these sweaty, shirtless bodies. I bet when you get home, when you're in the shower, you think about—"

"Benjamin!" Ronny snapped loudly. "That's *enough*."

Ben stood up and stared down at his older brother, who was still tying his shoes. He leaned over so only Ronny could hear as he hissed, "You sick faggot."

Ronny pretended that he didn't hear. He felt that if he said anything, he would get violently ill. He felt like punching his brother.

They used to get along so well when they were younger. Before that life-changing day when he was fourteen years old, Ronny and Ben were inseparable. Ben had even asked people to call him "Benny" so that his name sounded closer to his older brother's. Now Ben was disclaiming any genealogy that the two boys shared.

Ronny waited for his brother to leave the locker room before he finally decided that his shoes were tied to perfection. He stood up, kept his head down, and walked out of the locker room.

Kurt did not speak to him until the coach had taken roll and they had started running. "I don't want to pry," he said softly, "but, if you ever want to talk, I'm here for you."

"You've known me for less than two days," said Ronny.

"Yeah, I know… But, when I'm around you, I feel this…connection, like we were made for each other, you know?" Ronny felt his heart beat faster.

Was Kurt saying what he thought he was saying…? "I mean, I've never felt this way around anyone else before. It's like I just know that we're going to be best friends, you know what I mean?"

Ronny nodded, not trusting himself to speak. So, Kurt was talking about friendship? Well, why was he expecting anything else?

"So," Kurt continued, completely oblivious to any alternate meaning his previous statements could have had, "if you ever want to talk, I'm here for you. Okay?"

"Yeah, thanks, Kurt. That really means a lot to me."

"I'll race you?"

Ronny shook his head. "No, not right now. I'm feeling a little…ill…"

"Because of your brother?"

One quick, sharp nod. "Yeah."

"It kind of sucks that they don't split up the P.E. classes by grade," said Kurt, trying to change the subject. "I mean, we all have to take the class at least one semester every year. They should split up the grades."

"Yeah," said Ronny, glad that the conversation had shifted away from him and his brother. "Yeah, that way, we don't have to put up with freshmen."

"Hey, do you have a cell phone?"

"What? Yeah, but it's back in the locker room…"

Kurt pulled out his phone. "What's your number?"

Chapter Three

RONNY COHEN WAS really, really, really happy. Not only did he go to school with the sexiest man alive and been declared his new best friend, but said sexy man had asked him for his cell phone number! It was Friday, two weeks after he had started at Dickson County High School. The moment Ronny was home, he ran upstairs to his room and turned on his computer. He pulled up his instant messaging program and immediately sent a message to his friend Steven, his former roommate at St. Paul's.

> RCohen854: Hey, Steven, you know that guy I was telling you about after my first day of school? Kurt Vaughn?
>
> AllSmiles9288: The one with the super hot dragon tattoo?
>
> RCohen854: Yeah, well, you're not going to believe this: He asked me for my phone number!!!
>
> AllSmiles9288: Seriously, man? That's awesome! So, you guys dating yet?
>
> RCohen854: Are you kidding? First off, my parents would *completely* disown me if I came home with a boyfriend. Second of all, I think he's straight. He's just an unconscious flirt.
>
> AllSmiles9288: Dude, can't wait until you're 18. Then your parents can't bitch at you anymore.
>
> RCohen854: Yeah, right. But, my phone's ringing. I think it's Kurt. I'll catch up with you later.

Ronny signed off the computer before picking up his phone. "Hello?"

"Hey, Ronny! It's Kurt! Hey, I was wondering if you wanted to sleep over at my house tonight. I bought this really awesome video game, and I have no one to play it with, so…"

Ronny tried to keep the excitement out of his voice. "Yeah, sure, that's cool."

After getting directions, Ronny hung up. An extra day to spend with Kurt? He resisted his sudden urge to cheer. Even if he could never have his crush as a boyfriend, that didn't mean they couldn't be friends, right?

Ronny practically danced out to his car.

Kurt hung up the phone, slightly confused. Ronny had seemed so excited to come over. He brushed it off, thinking that Ronny was just happy to have a friend at Dickson County High. Even though it had already been two weeks, Ronny didn't seem to have made many other friends.

He called his father to see when he was coming home. Unfortunately, his father was in the middle of performing a surgery, and he never got through to him. It didn't matter; he knew his father wouldn't mind if he had a friend over.

For as long as he could remember, Kurt had lived alone with his father. His parents had gotten divorced when he was two years old. His father had gotten full custody of Kurt, and his mother barely set aside time to see her son. The last time he had seen her was on her birthday two years ago.

As he was accustomed whenever his thoughts strayed to his mother, he did his best to push these unhappy thoughts from his mind before he set about making dinner.

It was strange, he thought. He and his father were so close, but Ronny and his family… From what little he had heard, Kurt gathered that their relationship was well past the breaking point. But, Ronny always seemed so happy. How had the strain not affected him? Maybe he was just really good at covering up the pain…?

What had Ronny done that had been horrible enough for his whole family to abandon him? No matter how hard he wracked his brain, Kurt couldn't think of a single thing that would make a mother and father completely disown their son.

Then again, he still had a hard time wrapping his mind around his mother and the divorce. She always looked so happy when she spoke of his father—how they had met, their first date… Always, this far-away look came into her eyes, and a look of pure bliss passed across her face. Why had they divorced, then? To this day, Kurt still could not get a straight answer out of either of his parents.

He jumped when he heard the doorbell, having been completely lost in his thoughts, and burnt himself on the frying pan. He turned down the stove and quickly ran to answer the door.

"Ronny!" he shouted, giving the slightly shorter man a big hug. "Hey, come on in. My dad's not here right now, I hope you don't mind. He was held up at the hospital doing some big surgery. Here, you can put your stuff in my room…"

Ronny stepped inside the small, one-story house and immediately felt at peace with the world. He hadn't been here for more than a minute and already this house felt more like a home than his own house did.

"It's just you and your dad here, then?" asked Ronny, following Kurt to his room.

"Yup, just me and my dad!"

Ronny put his stuff down on the floor and followed Kurt back to the kitchen. "It's funny," he said. "I imagined you having a big family."

Kurt laughed. "When I first saw you, I thought you were an only child."

Ronny stared at the stir fry sizzling in the frying pan. "Holy sh—smokes, man! I didn't know you could cook!"

Kurt wrapped his arms around Ronny. "I'm glad you caught yourself from cursing." He let go, and Ronny felt heat rush to his face. Kurt didn't notice. "Hey, why don't you go into the living room and watch TV? Dinner's almost ready. I'll bring it out in a few minutes."

Ronny walked into the other room in a daze. Even though he had watched Kurt hug all of his other friends and knew that Kurt just had a quixotic personality, even though he *knew* the hug meant nothing special, he couldn't help but wish…

No. You will stop this crush. Kurt is your friend, nothing else.

But still…

"Hey, Ronny," Kurt called from the other room. "You want a soda, or what?"

"Do you have any milk?" Ronny called back.

In the kitchen, Kurt wrinkled his nose. "Milk and stir fry? Gross!" To Ronny he shouted, "Yeah, I got it. Are you sure that's what you want, though? Because, seriously, milk is just…yuck!"

Ronny chuckled. "Each to his own."

"Ew…"

They ate dinner together on the floor in front of the television. Kurt took the time to teach Ronny how to eat with chopsticks, saying that eating Chinese food with a fork was heresy.

"How can it be heresy," Ronny snapped after several failed tries, "when you're not even *Chinese*?"

Kurt shrugged. "It's the rules, man. I didn't make them up. Here, you're holding it wrong again! Keep it balanced against your knuckle, like this…" Ronny felt a chill run up his spine as Kurt reached around his back to adjust the chopsticks. Kurt moved the chopsticks up and down for Ronny. "See how easy that is? Now, you try it!"

Ronny tried and failed to retrieve a piece of chicken from his plate. Kurt reached over and snatched the chicken off the plate.

"New rule!" said Kurt. "If you can't get it off your plate, I get to eat it!"

Ronny snorted. "What, you're going to starve me to death? Is that your new plan?"

Kurt scratched his head. "Hmm… I didn't think about it that way… Okay, okay, you win. I'll go get you a fork. But next time…don't think you'll be getting away with this!"

"Next time?"

"Yeah, sure, any time you want to come over, you're welcome. Although, I promise I won't make you eat non-Chinese food with chopsticks."

Ronny watched with a smile as Kurt paused in his ramblings to take a sip of his soda. He had fallen head over heels with this man he had known for less than a month. Kurt had cast aside the conformity rule of Dickson County High just to make a lone student happy, and Ronny really admired him, really trusted him. Out of everyone he knew, Ronny knew that Kurt would view him in the same way he always had if he knew…

Maybe he should tell him…

The phone rang, and Kurt swallowed his food. "Maybe it's my dad!" His eyes lit up at the mention of his father, and he picked up the phone. "Hello? Oh! Lauren! Hey! What's up? You—*what*? Hey, that's *awesome*! Yeah, I can't wait to see you, too! Hey, look, I've got a friend over right now—no, not Mitchell. Nah, that kid's not on my good list right now. Yeah, he's the one that never bathes. No, it's Ronny Cohen; remember I told you about him? So, I'll call you back later? All right, awesome. Yeah, I love you, too. Bye."

Kurt hung up the phone, a silly grin plastered across his face. "Sorry about that," he said to Ronny. "That was my girlfriend, Lauren."

Ronny could practically feel his blissful mood crashing to the ground. "Girlfriend?" he repeated hollowly. "I didn't know you had a girlfriend."

"Yeah," Kurt replied, obviously unaware of Ronny's depressed tone of voice. "She lives in California. We met at Guitar Camp last year. The long distance isn't really putting a strain on us, but she's coming to visit in a few weeks! How awesome is that?"

"That's really awesome." Even though Ronny knew he never had a chance with Kurt, he could almost literally hear his heart breaking in two. Besides, how could he *possibly* measure up to the caliber of someone from Cali-fucking-fornia? He came from a private school, not from white sand beaches and Hollywood pop icons. On that note, how could he even possibly measure up to a *girl*? He should have known Kurt was straight, but…just the way he…

Ronny stared blankly at the wall, trying to process this information as Kurt prattled on and on about Lauren. With as much as Kurt liked to talk, Ronny couldn't help but wonder why he had never mentioned Lauren before…

No, Ronny scolded himself. *My heart's already been broken once tonight over Kurt. I won't try to fool myself into thinking something was there, that something could have happened between us.*

"…and she has the most *gorgeous* eyes. They're, like, the exact same color as the ocean. The only person I've ever seen with prettier eyes is you, Ronny."

Ronny wouldn't have been able to stop the blush from flooding his cheeks even if he wanted to. Once again, Kurt had no idea how much sway his words held over Ronny.

"Er… Thanks, Kurt. Y—You have very pretty eyes, too…"

Kurt smiled. "Hey, thanks, man! I got them from my mom. They look blue, but if you look closer, they're almost grey."

Ronny nodded. He had noticed. He had also noticed that they turned fully grey when Kurt wore black. And that Kurt's black hair was actually dark brown. And that when the sun hit his hair just right, it was framed in a halo of gold…

Kurt was talking again. "But, I mean, your eyes, they're made of magic or something! It's almost as if when God created you, he took your iris and a marker and made one stripe of green, one stripe of yellow, one stripe of green…all the way around your eye. They're so pretty…"

Ronny willed his blush to fade. How could he fall out of love with the man who continuously showered compliments on his visage?

He needed…

"Hey, Kurt?" said Ronny softly. "Could you stop doing that?"

"Doing what?"

Ronny didn't know how to put it into words. "Could you stop...complimenting me? You're... It's almost like you're flirting with me."

Kurt stared at him, confused. "Ronny... Are you homo—"

Ronny felt his blood run cold and his stomach plummet. *Here it comes... He's never going to talk to me again...*

"—phobic?"

Ronny almost started laughing. For all the intelligence Kurt had, he sure could be dumb as a brick at times. "No, I'm not homophobic. Quite the opposite, actually."

Kurt unconsciously scooted closer to Ronny. "Well, what's the problem, then? Why can't I compliment you? You're a really good-looking guy. Why be ashamed?"

Oh, if only you knew...

"I just...feel uncomfortable, you know?" His brain began to fog as Kurt came even closer. *Damn him... He practically radiates sexy.* "I mean, I appreciate you complimenting me, but it just makes me feel a little awkward."

Kurt pouted, and Ronny had to restrain himself from kissing his protruding bottom lip. "I can't help it," said Kurt. "I'm sorry, but...it's just part of my personality. I see something, and I just have to say whatever's on my mind. But...I'll try, I suppose. I mean, I *did* force *you* to stop cursing..."

"I—It's not that—"

Kurt turned his eyes toward Ronny, and they seemed colder than usual. "Well, then, what is it? What is it that you want from me?"

I want you to love me! Ronny wanted to scream. *I want to tell you that I love you!*

Instead, Ronny said, "I—I don't know..."

Kurt wrapped his arms around his new best friend. "Look, kiddo, I can't change my personality, no matter how hard I try. It was just how I was raised, you know? My dad always told me to say whatever's on my mind. He said that hesitation can lead to regret. I mean, yeah, I'm not going to tell a woman she's morbidly obese, but I can tell her that she's beautiful, right?"

Ronny nodded. A warm, tingling sensation was bubbling in his stomach as Kurt rubbed small circles along his spinal column. He subconsciously leaned closer to Kurt, toward the warmth he exuded.

"I can't help it," Kurt continued. "It's bred in me. Honestly, I've been restraining myself a bit. I didn't want to scare you off when I first met you, if you thought I was gay or something. But, in all honesty...ever since I first sat by you at lunch..."

Ronny's stomach did a flip-flop as he felt Kurt resting his head against his shoulder. He spoke softer now that he was closer to his ear, his voice a sensual purr.

"Ever since I first met you…I've wanted to tell you how beautiful your eyes are…how your haircut frames your face perfectly…how those grey highlights stand out beautifully against your blond hair and pale skin…how the smell of peaches in your shampoo contrasts almost sumptuously against the cinnamon scent of your aftershave."

Ronny had never wanted to kiss anyone as badly as he wanted to kiss Kurt now. He felt himself leaning in, his eyes fluttering closed…

The phone rang, and Kurt extracted himself from Ronny. Ronny felt cold with the loss of contact. He started to curse the interruption before realizing that it had stopped him from doing something he would probably regret later.

"Hello? Oh, Dad! Hey! You got my message? It's all right if he stays over, then? Awesome, thanks! How was the surgery? Oh, that's good, then. When do you think you'll be home? Oh… No, no, I understand. I'll see you tomorrow, then. Yeah. Awesome. I love you, too, Dad."

Kurt hung up the phone and grinned sheepishly. "Gee, I can't get this phone to stop ringing, can I? What can I say? I'm popular!" He stood up and stretched. "All right, let me get these dishes washed, and then I'm going to kick your ass in snowboarding. You want to hook up the game? You should probably get in as much extra practice as possible. I'm a beast at snowboarding."

Ronny had trouble sleeping that night. He had been raised up on a metaphorical pedestal after he had beaten Kurt five times in a row. He failed to mention that he had the same video game at home, preferring instead to have beginner's luck.

The mood of the rest of the evening had been light and happy, but as Ronny was getting ready for bed, Kurt had taken the time to call Lauren back. As Ronny listened to Kurt and how happy he was with her, he felt guilty for ever thinking that he had a chance with Kurt…and felt even guiltier when he realized how happy it would make him to tear the two of them apart. He felt jealous, knowing that Kurt would always have thousands of girls to choose from while he would, in all probability, be alone for a good portion of his life.

He pretended to sleep, his sleeping bag pulled over his head, and tried to block out Kurt's voice. Even though Kurt had gone into the other room, Ronny could still hear his voice, loud and clear.

He pulled the sleeping bag even farther over his head as he felt the beginnings of a tear working its way down his cheek.

How could he feel this way? *How*? He had known Kurt for only two weeks, and he sure as hell didn't believe in love at first sight! Hell, after his parents shipped him off to a boarding school, he wasn't sure if he believed in love at all!

But when Kurt looked at him…he felt as if he were soaring high above the clouds, dancing with the stars, walking hand-in-hand with the Milky Way. Kurt accepted him for who he was. Ronny was sure, in fact, that even if Kurt knew he were gay, it wouldn't change anything between them, but… he was afraid…

Afraid to lose what had never been his to begin with.

"What's wrong with me?" he whispered as more tears rushed down his cheeks. He heard Kurt walk into the room. He hastily wiped the tears away and sank even further into his sleeping bag.

Kurt hung up the phone with Lauren. She always made him feel giddy and happy. He realized that their relationship could never last, that her living so far away would eventually put a huge strain on what they had, but he couldn't help living in the moment. Besides, she was coming to see him in two weeks!

Kurt honestly didn't even view Lauren as his girlfriend. He viewed her as more of a really good friend who he would bring to the movies and pay for her ticket and popcorn. They had never kissed, and Kurt frankly didn't care if they ever *did* kiss. Sex was entirely out of the question; he felt it would be way too awkward afterward.

Walking back into his room, he heard faint sniffling. He watched Ronny moving deeper into the sleeping bag. Wondering if perhaps this was his outlet for the strain between him and his family members, Kurt gently pulled the sleeping bag away from Ronny's face. "Hey, kiddo, what's the matter?"

Ronny looked shocked for a moment, embarrassed even. He wiped hastily at his tears. "Nothing." His voice cracked, and another tear ran down his face.

Kurt sat down on the floor and pulled Ronny into his lap, wrapping his arms tightly around him. For once, Ronny hugged back. Kurt was so concerned as to why his friend was crying that he didn't even realize the warm gush flowing through his stomach nor the quickening of his heart as Ronny squeezed him even tighter.

"Something is obviously wrong," said Kurt softly. "It's okay. You can trust me."

"I—I do trust you," Ronny whimpered. "It's just that…I can't…"

Kurt felt himself getting angry. "Can't what?" he demanded. "You just said that you trust me! You can tell me anything, and I won't think any less of you! Here, I'll tell you something about me: When I was eight years old, I walked in on my parents having sex. They divorced when I was two."

Ronny's tears stopped from the shock of what Kurt had told him. "Wh—What?"

"There," said Kurt haughtily. "I told you something embarrassing about my life. I've never told *anyone* that before, not even my dad. What could be more embarrassing than that? And you don't think any less of me, do you?"

Ronny shook his head slowly. "No, but…that was an accident. I'm… There's something wrong with me."

Kurt was confused. "What? Like, you have a tail or something?"

"No, not physically… It's psychological, or so they say… I really don't understand…" He pressed himself closer into Kurt's chest. He hadn't been hugged like this since he was a child. Not even his sister dared to hug him— even though she was the most accepting, it didn't mean that she refrained from turning the other cheek from time to time.

"Please, Kurt…" Ronny's head was buried in Kurt's shoulder, so his voice came out muffled and distorted. "Please, let's not talk about it now. Please…"

Holy shit, Kurt thought to himself as he wrapped his arms even tighter around his new friend. *What the hell did they do to this kid? What lies have they been feeding him?*

Without thinking, Kurt placed a light kiss on top of Ronny's head.

They fell asleep together like that.

Chapter Four

Ronny Cohen awoke with a crick in his neck. The muscles in his right shoulder and lower back were uncomfortably stiff, and it hurt to move. He blushed when he realized that he and Kurt had fallen asleep in each other's arms on the floor. He extracted himself from the other's limbs and made his way to the bathroom to brush his teeth.

Kurt woke up slowly when he heard Ronny moving around the house. He let memories of the night before wash over him and felt confused. Accompanying the feeling of sorrow he felt for the boy came the realization that he had felt aroused after Ronny had fallen asleep in his arms. He tried to pass off the feeling as just being tired and that Ronny had felt so warm...

He sat up and stretched. His arm tingled painfully, and he realized that Ronny must have been lying on it. He waited until the blood was flowing back into his arm before he got up to make breakfast.

Ronny stepped out of the shower and slowly got dressed. After he had toweled his hair dry, he made his way into the kitchen and was greeted with the smell of bacon and eggs.

"Good morning, sunshine!" said Kurt cheerfully. He had changed out of the clothes he had slept in and into lounge pants. His blue plaid pants hung dangerously low over his hips, his dragon tattoo open for the world to see.

"G—Good morning," Ronny stuttered as he ogled at the tattoo.

"What do you want to do today?" Kurt asked as he handed Ronny a plate and a glass of orange juice. He pointed to the kitchen table, and Ronny sat down and waited for Kurt to finish cooking breakfast.

Ronny shifted uncomfortably in his chair. His eyes were locked where Kurt's tanned skin met lighter skin…right around where the bathing suit would be…

"Hellooo," called Kurt, waving his hand in front of Ronny's eyes. "Earth to Ronny… HEY! You awake?"

Ronny forced himself to look up into Kurt's eyes. "Oh, yeah, sorry. I'm still…sleepy…"

Kurt laughed. "Yeah, I could tell. Hey, you want to go see a movie? Wait… No, I don't have any money. Umm…"

"We could always…stay here…"

That way you won't have to put on a shirt any time soon.

Ronny blushed the moment that thought passed through his mind, and it didn't help that his eyes were glued on the tail of the dragon as it ran in spirals around Kurt's navel.

Kurt dished food onto Ronny's plate and sat down across from him, and the dragon's tail disappeared from view. Ronny instead focused on the head that wrapped around over the right shoulder, and the flame that raced across his toned chest…

"Ronny?" Kurt asked. "Are you all right?"

"Uh, yeah, sorry." Ronny felt mortified. He had been caught openly staring at Kurt twice in the past five minutes. He quickly began eating in an attempt to cover up his embarrassment.

"You were looking at my tattoo?"

Ronny figured there must be an art to making a statement while simultaneously asking a question.

Seemingly without realizing the effect his actions had on poor Ronny, Kurt took his right index finger and traced the outline of the flame, starting near his right collarbone and following it in a delicious curve around his left breast. He looked up quickly when he heard Ronny choking on his orange juice.

"Whoa, man, you okay?" Kurt leapt up from his chair and quickly thumped him on the back. "You all right? You breathing?"

Ronny coughed a few more times before answering, "Yeah, I'm all right. Thanks a million, Kurt." At least he could pass off his blush as an aftereffect of choking instead of from watching that hand tracing that gorgeous body… He blushed even harder when he found himself wishing that it had been *his* hand running across that tattoo…

The front door opened, and Kurt rushed out of the room. Ronny stared at the spot where Kurt had been a mere second before. He had the odd feeling of having been watching a cartoon, as if Kurt's outline were still in the air before him.

"Dad!" Ronny heard Kurt shout from the other room. "It's great that you're home! I want you to meet someone!"

Ronny stood up and made his way out into the adjacent living room. Kurt stood beaming up at his father, his arms wrapped tightly around him. Mr. Vaughn patiently pulled at Kurt's arms until they loosened up enough for him to breathe.

Kurt finally noticed Ronny had followed him in. "Oh, right, Dad... This is my new best friend, Ronny Cohen."

"It's so great to finally meet you," said Mr. Vaughn, extending his hand out toward Ronny. "Kurt has told me so much about you. As you might have noticed, this boy never shuts up."

Kurt grinned sheepishly. "Well, there's so much to tell! Take life by the...however that phrase goes... Whatever. Ronny, this is my dad, Peter Vaughn."

"It's very nice to meet you, sir," said Ronny.

Kurt looked very similar to his father. They were the same height and had the same color hair and body shape. However, while Mr. Vaughn was pale like Ronny, Kurt had very tan skin, like creamy coffee.

"Dad, do you want some breakfast?"

Pete Vaughn nodded. "Yeah, I haven't eaten since I left yesterday morning. We were so backed up on surgeries, it was crazy! And then I'm going to bed. You boys been having fun?"

"Yes!" said Kurt immediately, practically skipping into the kitchen to fix breakfast for his father.

"I wasn't really asking you, Kurt," said Pete Vaughn. "You could have fun with a blade of grass." He winked at Ronny, and Ronny laughed. "Hey, Ronny, has Kurt invited you camping this weekend?"

"Ah!" shouted Kurt from the kitchen. "I totally forgot to ask! Ronny, do you want to go camping with me and my dad next weekend? We always go around this time of year. It's a nice, little, secluded place out by a lake, and there are hardly any bugs... Tons of squirrels, though, and they throw acorns at your head. Last year, we went with Keith and Mitchell, and they were smoking and—"

"You're not still friends with them, right?" Peter asked hastily. "Because, honestly, I don't want them burning down the tent again this year."

Kurt laughed. "Yeah, they're no longer in the picture. I don't even think they noticed, those assholes."

Ronny stared. "They burned down the tent?"

Peter nodded, his mouth drawing into a thin, angry line. "They sure did. That's why we have to share a tent this year. Hopefully, I'll have bought an extra tent by next year, but I kept forgetting..." He shoved his last bite of toast into his mouth and announced that he was going to bed and to try to keep the noise level down.

"All right, Dad," said Kurt. "You want me to wake you up at five?"

Peter shook his head. "Nah, I don't go back in until nine. I'll get up around seven. If I'm not up by eight, come get me."

Ronny didn't get home until nearly four thirty. He expected his parents to ignore him when he came in, but they were immediately on him, almost as if they had been waiting right next to the door for his return.

"Where have you been?" Margaret Cohen demanded.

Ronny looked slightly taken aback. "I told Georgina to tell you where I was going... Didn't she mention it?"

"She did," snarled Ronald, Sr. "That's exactly why we're so worried. She said—" He lowered his voice, as if afraid that someone would overhear him. "She *said* that you went over to a—a *boy's* house."

Ronny laughed hollowly. "All right. So? You don't yell at *Benny* for going over to *his* guy friends' houses."

"Yeah, but he's not—you know!" Margaret Cohen looked absolutely terrified of saying the "g" word.

"Gay?" Ronny said, glaring angrily at his parents when they flinched. "He's just a *friend*, Mom. Just because I'm gay doesn't mean I'll go around fucking every man on the planet. Heteroes don't do that, do they? You don't see two people suddenly jumping each other in the middle of the supermarket, *do you*? Besides that, he's *straight*!"

"It doesn't matter if he's *seems* straight," Ronny's father snapped. "You never know—"

"For your information," Ronny replied coldly, "he has a girlfriend. Her name is Lauren, and he loves her more than life itself. I'm going up to my room now. Don't follow me."

When he got to his room, he locked the door behind him and threw himself onto his bed...and cried.

"Good Monday!" said Kurt cheerfully, catching up with Ronny as the blond stepped out of his car. "Did you have a good—*holy shit*! What happened to you?"

Ronny grinned sheepishly as he rubbed the cut under his lip. "I wasn't watching where I was going, and I ran into a door…"

"…Liar."

Ronny sighed. "I know," he said softly. "I was practicing. Did it sound convincing?"

"Well, yeah, but…what the hell happened?"

Without any warning, Ronny launched himself into Kurt's chest, burying his face in his shirt and wrapping his arms around his torso. "My parents and I got into a fight. And then Ben got into the fight… But if you think I look bad, just wait until you see my brother…"

Ronny jumped when he felt something wet soak through his hair. He pulled back from the brunette slightly to look at his face and was confused when he saw the tears. "Kurt, what's wrong—?"

Kurt pulled him back into a deep hug. "You shouldn't have to suffer like that. No family should be that broken apart…"

Slowly, Ronny raised his head up. Being only a couple inches shorter than Kurt, his lips didn't have far to go before they reached their destination: They kissed away a tear that had trickled all the way down to Kurt's chin. "Please don't worry about it, Kurt," he said softly. "I hate to see you upset."

Kurt looked as if he didn't even notice the kiss. "Trust me, kiddo, it hurts me a hundred times more to see you so upset every day. One of these days, you **have** to tell me what this is all about. I don't think I can take it much longer…"

Benji, who had gotten a ride from one of his friends, stopped suddenly as he passed by Ronny's car. Had he just seen Ronny kissing Kurt—in *public*? He felt anger well up in his chest. "Ronny!" he shouted.

Ronny blushed, knowing exactly how much of the scene his brother had just witnessed. "Benny, it's not what you think—"

"Just get to your fucking class," Benji snarled, turning quickly on his heel and stalking up to the building.

"You're going to let him talk to you like that?" Kurt questioned with a quirked eyebrow. "He's your little brother…"

"Yeah, I know… Did you see his eye?"

Kurt nodded. "You did that?"

"Yeah… I didn't mean to, though… It was just kind of, you know, a *reaction*. My fist just soared through the air… But then he busted my lip, so I guess we're even." Kurt saw straight through Ronny's attempt at a joke, especially when the blond hung his head like a dog that had been kicked.

Kurt's eyes lit up suddenly. "Hey, you got any tests today, kiddo?"

"No… Why?"

His keys were gone and Kurt was in the front seat of the convertible before he even had a chance to bat an eyelash.

"Kurt, what the hell are you doing?"

"Get in the car, kiddo."

"But—"

"No buts," argued Kurt. "Just get in the damn car already."

Ronny sighed but gave in anyway. He climbed into the passenger seat and buckled as Kurt revved the engine. Ronny's favorite band, Umbrellas Without a Handle, blared through the speakers. Kurt raised an eyebrow at the lyrics.

"*Touch me here, touch me there, touch, touch, everywhere. Please, baby, please, let's keep this going…*"

Ronny blushed. "It's about getting a massage, I promise! We just came in at a really…awkward part of the song…"

Kurt laughed, enjoying watching Ronny blush. He grabbed Ronny's wrist as the blond reached to change the station. "No, don't, it's got a nice beat to it."

"*Oh, baby, you make me feel so good. I'd pay a hell of a lot more than $40 an hour just to feel you do this to me that way, this way, every—every—every niiiiiight!*"

"Who is this, anyway?" Kurt asked once they had left the school premises.

"Umbrellas Without a Handle," answered Ronny. "They're my favorite band."

"I'll bet," said Kurt with a wink.

"*My Sally… My massage therapist!*"

"So, where are we going?" Ronny asked once the song was over. He felt nervous as Kurt took his car onto the interstate. He was already worried about the wellbeing of his car, as well as getting caught skipping school, that he didn't need the added stress of having someone else driving his precious car on the interstate. If anything happened to his car, he knew his parents wouldn't put a dime toward it. He was already lucky enough to have inherited the car from his uncle; he didn't need any bad luck to come his way.

Kurt watched Ronny tensing up as the speedometer crept toward 70 miles per hour. "Ronny," he said softly, placing his right hand on Ronny's thigh. "Calm down. I won't hurt your car."

Ronny sighed. "I know. It's just that if there's a freak accident of some sort…"

"I would feel even worse than you would, trust me." Kurt let go of Ronny's leg and put both of his hands on the steering wheel. He saw Ronny visibly relax a little the second his skin touched the leather wheel. He sighed. This boy was just *too tense*… Maybe they were better off staying at the school…

An image of Benji's livid expression as he caught the two of them hugging passed through his mind. Unconsciously, his foot pressed harder on the gas pedal.

Ronny whimpered. "K—Kurt… Your speed… Please…"

Kurt gasped when he realized he was going over 90 miles per hour. "Ah!" He took his foot off the gas and waited for the car to slow back down to the speed limit. "I'm really sorry, Ronny! Damn, this car…you barely press down on the gas, and…"

"Yeah, I know. It takes some getting used to." Ronny pointed both air conditioning vents toward his face and rolled down the window. He was panting after that little "adventure."

"Are we almost there?" he moaned, afraid of getting sick.

Kurt felt a twinge of guilt in his stomach and resolved to remain more attentive on the road and less on ornery little brothers. "Yeah, we're nearly there. It's at the next exit."

"What? There's nothing *at* the next exit, except the mall… We're not going to the mall, are we? You said the other day that you were broke…"

"I did some favors for my dad yesterday while he was at work, and he gave me fifty bucks. But, honestly, who goes to the mall to spend money?"

Ronny snorted and rolled up his window. "Well, don't beg money from me when you—" He paused when he felt his phone vibrate in his pocket. He glanced at the caller ID and winced when he saw "Mom." He flipped open the phone with a tentative, "Hello?" He quickly pulled the phone away from his ear when she started yelling. "What? Mom, no! I'm at *school*! Where else do you think I would be? What? No, Benji's a *liar*! I was *not*! Mom, look, the bell's about to ring, and I'm going to get in trouble. No, I'm hanging up the phone now. Bye." He snapped his phone shut angrily and shoved it back into his pocket.

Kurt took his hand off the steering wheel once more and entwined his fingers with Ronny's. As they had just gotten off the interstate, Ronny didn't tense up as much when Kurt's hand left the steering wheel. Instead, Ronny squeezed Kurt's hand back tightly.

"You still coming camping with us this weekend?" Kurt asked.

Ronny subconsciously rubbed at the cut on his lip with the tip of his tongue. "Yeah, I think…I think I should get away for a weekend…"

Kurt squeezed his hand even tighter, willing the weekend to come sooner so that the blond could have some peace of mind, if only for a few days…

To ease Ronny's nerves, Kurt parked farther away from the mall than he usually would have, in order to avoid parking next to anyone. He made sure the doors were locked before handing Ronny the keys. He slipped his hand back into Ronny's, their fingers entwining.

I can't take much more of this, Ronny thought as he pressed himself up against Kurt. *I can't take his flirting with me and knowing that I can never be with him. He's going to drive me over the edge, and I don't know if I'll ever be able to get back.*

Chapter Five

Ronny Cohen had not bothered to tell his mother that he was going camping with his best friend for a weekend. In fact, he had not even bothered to tell her that his best friend's father had cancelled on them at the last minute, as he had to work the next morning.

When Kurt had first told him of Peter Vaughn's cancellation, Ronny had been extremely happy. Just him and Kurt, all alone in the middle of the woods together…in the same tent, no less. Then, he realized that this was probably one of the worst bouts of bad luck he had run across in *ages*. No one was there to stop him if he did something…stupid.

I can't have Kurt! he coerced himself time and time again. *We have no chance together, so give up this stupid little crush!*

He kicked his bed angrily, trying to relieve some of the pent-up stress he was under. He picked up his phone and called his friend Steven.

"Hey, yo, Ronny, my man!" said Steven, picking up after the second ring. "I am *so* glad you called! You have no idea how boring it is here—oh, wait, you do."

Ronny laughed. Steven continuously "forgot" that they had been room-mates for three years at St. Paul's. "Yeah, well, it's getting pretty complicated up here," said Ronny. "I can't get over my crush on Kurt! And now his dad's not even going camping with us…"

"I feel your pain, man," said Steven. Ronny knew he did. Steven's parents had caught him making out with a girl and quickly shipped him off to St.

Paul's. Thinking about it, most of the kids at St. Paul's were not there of their own will…

"So, are there any new girls at that school?"

"Damn it, I *wish*!" said Steven testily. "Out of the 300 students, only about 50 of them are girls. And out of those, like, 40 are lesbians! It's not fair! How do they expect us to pass the time in a dump like this? I mean, we can't even go off campus."

"You could just switch to the other side, you know," Ronny joked.

"Don't tempt me," said Steven, actually sounding serious. "You have no idea how close I am. It's so hard to get off in here! I just want *someone to make out with!*"

Ronny laughed when he heard Steven punch the wall. "Careful there, buddy, or else you'll end up indebted to the school. And at least you have 300 people to choose from. My heart's chosen one man, and it won't let go, no matter how many times I tell it that Kurt is straight and totally out of my league."

"Hey, man, cheer up! If I'm thinking about turning gay, *anyone* could turn gay, you know what I mean?"

"…You're not helping."

"Oh, right, sorry. Look, just…I don't know. Maybe it will hurt less with time?"

"…You're terrible with advice. You know that, right?"

"Hey," said Steven defensively, "you're the one who called me. You knew exactly what you were getting into when you dialed my number. Remember the last time I gave you advice? I told you to play video games all night instead of studying for your math final."

"Yeah, I ignored your advice then, too."

Steven laughed. "Good thing. Okay, here's my second shot at advice: Don't have sex with him."

"That's not advice; that's common sense, you dolt!"

"Oh… Is it really? Hmm. I lack common sense then. Oh, hey, I've got to get to class in a couple minutes. Call me when you get back from your…trip. Just, don't tell me any of the juicy details. I'm sexually frustrated enough as it is here."

"Yeah, yeah, whatever, Steven. If you stop thinking about your libido long enough to think with your brain, you might actually be able to give out decent advice."

"Yeah, but I don't see that happening any time in the near future."

Ronny shook his head exasperatedly as he hung up his phone. He picked up his bag and his pillow and headed out to his car, surprised that his parents didn't try to stop him. He hadn't spoken to either his mother or father in nearly a week. He shuddered as he remembered their conversation, subconsciously pushing harder on the gas pedal in his anger.

"Benjamin told us that he saw you making out with a boy in the student parking lot!" Mrs. Margaret Cohen shrieked the moment Ronny walked through the doorway.

"Mom, you already called me about this!" Ronny said exasperatedly. "I told it to you then, and I'll tell it to you now: I was not making out with anyone! I promise! And tell Benny to mind his own fucking business!"

"Don't use that tone of voice, Ronald," Mr. Cohen scolded. "I forbid you from seeing this boy ever again!"

Ronny laughed tonelessly. "We have classes together. How am I supposed to—?"

"What's his name?" demanded his father as he pulled his cell phone out of his pocket. "I'll call the school right now and get your schedule changed."

"Dad, that's not—"

His mother cut him off. "Ronald, do you know why we sent you to St. Paul's? It wasn't just to cure your—"

"Being gay is not a fucking disease!"

She continued as if she hadn't heard a word he had said. "—ailment. It was to immerse you in a society of young teenagers all seeking a path of devotion and righteousness. We had been hoping that some of that would have rubbed off on you, but we were gravely mistaken."

"So what are you going to do?" Ronny spat coldly. "Are you going to send me back to St. Paul's? Because, trust me, lady, I wasn't the only queer on campus." He stormed up the stairs and slammed his door shut. The noise echoed down the hall and into the foyer where his parents stood, stunned.

His mother was quick to tell anyone who stood still long enough about her deep roots in Catholicism. It had taken her husband by surprise when he found that he had not only married Margaret Downs but also the Lord God Almighty. Not being one for religion, Ronald Sr. had begrudgingly accepted his wife's religion as his own.

Ronny sighed. It was hard enough for his parents to accept his sexual preference without the complications of religion, but with his mother hiding with her prejudices behind the protective force of the Bible, Ronny couldn't fathom his mother ever accepting him for who he was. His father was different, though—not that he was any more accepting. He didn't bother to pretend to hold up religion as a shield but flat out refused to believe that any son of his would turn out "that way."

Ronny glanced down at his speedometer and quickly took his foot off the gas. He grimaced when he realized that he had reached Kurt's house in nearly half the time it usually took. He was genuinely surprised that he hadn't been pulled over.

Kurt answered the door mere seconds after Ronny rang the doorbell. Ronny nearly fell over backward with the force of Kurt's hug.

"Come on!" said Kurt excitedly. "Let's get your stuff into my car so we can go!"

Ronny laughed. Kurt's excitement reminded him of a child inside of a candy store. He grabbed Ronny's stuff from the back seat and threw it into his truck before Ronny even noticed Kurt had released him from the hug.

Peter Vaughn walked outside wearing nothing but blue jeans. He had a cup of coffee in his hands, and his hair stuck out in odd directions as if he had just woken up from a nap.

"Kurt!" Mr. Vaughn yelled after his son. "You weren't thinking of leaving before saying good bye, were you?"

"Of course not!" said Kurt. He ran over to his father and wrapped his arms tightly around him. "How could I forget to say good bye to my dear old dad?" He kissed him on the cheek. "Bye, Dad!" He quickly let go and practically flew into the driver's seat of the truck.

Peter Vaughn made his way over to Ronny and shook his hand. "Have a great time, Ronny. And try to keep Kurt out of trouble."

"I'll try," said Ronny with a laugh.

The campsite was about two hours away. Ronny had brought along his CDs and was currently trying to get Kurt addicted to indie.

"I don't know," said Kurt. "There's just too much piano and not enough electric guitar. It's not my style."

"How can you not love this?" Ronny asked, turning up the volume. "Trust me, I'll get you converted yet. Just you wait."

Kurt rolled his eyes. "I can't wait."

The tent was pitched within half an hour of arriving at the campsite. Ronny, who had never been camping before, was more of a hindrance than a help. A tear of frustration nearly worked its way from his eye when the entire tent came down directly onto Kurt's head—twice.

"Hey, kiddo, relax!" said Kurt, laughing as he tried to disentangle himself from the tent. "Look, I can probably get this set up by myself... Why don't you go gather wood for the fire?"

"O—Okay..."

Ronny jumped when he felt Kurt wrapping his arms around him from behind.

"Hey, what's wrong?" Kurt asked, his lips mere millimeters from Ronny's ear. "You seem so depressed all of the sudden..."

Ronny smiled. "No, it's childish, really. I just...for a moment there, I found myself thinking, 'I can't do anything right.' You know how it is... How you get depressed for one moment, and in hindsight, it seems so childish."

Kurt's arms tightened even more, and Ronny found it hard to breathe. "You can do **anything**. You want to keep helping me set up the tent?"

"You serious?"

"Uh... Well..."

Ronny laughed. "Yeah, yeah, all right. I can take a hint. I'll go get the firewood and get out of your hair." Softly, he said, "Thank you. That really meant a lot."

Kurt finally let go and ruffled Ronny's hair. "Any time, kiddo."

Even after the tent had been pitched and the wood had been gathered, it was only two o'clock in the afternoon.

"Do you want to go swimming?" Kurt asked. "There's a lake right down the road, about a two minute's walk."

"Um... All right..."

Despite the heat of the day, the water felt cool against their skin. Kurt immediately waded out toward deeper water. Ronny followed at a slower pace, wary of seaweed and fish, jumping every time something brushed against his leg.

"Oh, quit being such a girl," Kurt teased with a laugh. "Seaweed isn't going to hurt you."

"I know it's not going to hurt me," said Ronny tersely, "but it's still disgusting." He grimaced when he saw the water turn cloudy from the dirt being churned up by his feet. "There are showers around here, right?"

Kurt rolled his eyes. "Of course there are showers. But, just try to relax, Ronny. People come out here all the time and test to make sure this water is safe. There'd be signs posted if there was anything dangerous lurking in the shadows."

Ronny willed himself to relax. He wasn't used to swimming in anything that didn't have dangerously high levels of chlorine…and he *definitely* wasn't used to sharing any body of water with nonhumans. He grimaced as he felt a fish brush up against his leg.

"If you keep moving around, the fish will stay away," Kurt reasoned.

The dragon's head bobbed up and down below the surface as Kurt tread water. It was…hypnotizing almost, and Ronny fell into a semi-trance watching it. It wasn't until a large wave of water cascaded over his head did he snap out of it.

"Kuuurt," he whined, wiping the water out of his eyes. "That was gross…"

Kurt laughed. "Sorry, it won't happen again."

A mischievous twinkle shone in Ronny's eye. He swam closer and closer to Kurt before dunking the unsuspecting brunette's head under the water. Kurt came up sputtering, casting an angry eye at Ronny.

"You little jerk face," Kurt said with a laugh. "You'd better run before I retaliate!"

"How can I run?" Ronny said, smirking. "I'm in water!"

Kurt came closer to Ronny. "Well, you'd better find a way, and quickly!" He lunged to dunk Ronny, but the latter had already disappeared under the water. He gasped when he felt Ronny pulling his leg, successfully pulling him back under the water.

Their water fight seemed to last a lot longer than it actually did. Kurt floated along on his back, panting from laughing so hard.

"So, you finally over your fear of lake water?" Kurt taunted.

Ronny rolled his eyes. "It wasn't a fear. It's a general dislike for things that are unclean."

"Okay, Mr. Obsessive Compulsive."

Ronny stuck his tongue out at Kurt. "Do you want to go in, then? Mr. Obsessive Compulsive would really like a shower right about now. I want to get this fish poop out of my hair."

Kurt snorted. "All right, all right…"

The rest of the evening went by peacefully, the two boys laughing and joking with each other. When the sun set, Kurt lit the fire, and they made s'mores. Ronny giggled as Kurt devoured his, making a huge mess.

"Uh, Kurt, you have some…marshmallow on the side of your mouth."

Kurt reached up and wiped the goo away with his index finger. Ronny nearly blushed as Kurt's pink tongue reached out and licked the marshmallow from his finger. He grinned. "Hey, thanks, man! Oh, and you have chocolate across your chin. Let me get it…" He used his middle finger to wipe the chocolate from Ronny's chin before sliding the appendage into his mouth.

"Mmm…"

Ronny honestly didn't know if that sound had come from him or from Kurt.

Kurt finished his s'more and yawned. "Well, I think I'm ready to go to bed. Do you want to stay up a little bit longer, or should I put out the fire?"

"Go ahead and put out the fire," said Ronny. "I think I'll go to bed, too."

Once the fire had been completely doused, the two headed into the tent. Without warning, Kurt stripped down to his boxers.

"You don't mind if I sleep like this, do you?" said Kurt. "I mean, it's kind of hot outside…"

"N—No," Ronny said, ashamed of his stutter. He cleared his throat and tried again. "No, it's no problem. Why would I mind?"

Kurt shrugged. "Most of my guy friends flip when they stay over at my house and make me put on pajamas. I just get so hot when I sleep… It's easier just to sleep in my boxers, you know? Besides, at least I don't sleep in the nude."

Ronny laughed before putting on a pair of Christmas pajamas and a grey T-shirt. "Yeah, just don't make fun of my pajamas. They were all that was clean, okay?"

Kurt snorted and began to sing "Jingle Bells" under his breath. Ronny picked up his pillow and bopped Kurt over the head with it. Kurt snatched the pillow away from Ronny and used it to hit the slightly shorter boy across the back. Ronny grabbed Kurt's pillow and used it to block Kurt's second hit.

Fifteen minutes later, the two boys were lying flat on their backs, the pillows lying forgotten beside them. Kurt was asleep within seconds, stretched out across both boys' sleeping bags. Ronny sighed, and, not wanting to wake him, lay down next to him and fell asleep.

When Ronny woke up the next morning, he realized that he had snuggled up to Kurt and had his head on the brunette's chest. He was mortified when he heard Kurt chuckle and say, "Comfy?"

Ronny leapt back. "Kurt! I'm so sorry! I don't know—"

Kurt waved his hand. "Relax, kiddo. You were sleeping. It's not like you can control what you do while you sleep. And it's not like you molested me or anything."

Ronny paled, thinking of what else *could* have happened during the night. Damn Kurt! Why did he have to be so damn sexy?

"Do you want to go hiking today?" asked Kurt as he got up and put on a pair of blue jeans.

"Hiking sounds…marvelous."

After they had showered and dressed, Kurt led Ronny to the dirt paths that wound through a great expanse of woods.

"If we're really quiet," said Kurt, "we might see some wildlife that doesn't include squirrels. My dad and I saw some deer one time, and Dad swears that he saw a mountain lion. I think he was just pulling my leg, though."

Halfway up the mountain, Kurt paused and pointed off into the trees. When Ronny opened his mouth to ask what he was pointing at, Kurt placed a finger over his lips, signaling for them to be quiet. Ronny gasped when he finally saw the mother deer and her child standing side by side, getting a drink from the river.

"They're so beautiful," Ronny said, his voice softer than a whisper.

Kurt grinned as he watched Ronny's reaction. He was sure that this is what he must have looked like the first time he had seen deer in the wild.

After several minutes, the deer took off running into the woods. Ronny continued to stare at the spot where the deer had been until Kurt pulled on Ronny's wrist.

"Come on, kiddo. We can't stand around here all day…"

Ronny followed Kurt the rest of the way up the mountain in a daze. "Deer," he said softly. "Real live deer…"

When they reached the top of the incline, Kurt laughed when he heard Ronny gasp again. From here, they could see over the tops of the trees for miles around. There were clouds overhead, and the few rays of sunshine that broke through shone like spotlights across the treetops. It truly was a beautiful sight…

"I wish I had a camera," said Ronny breathlessly as a flock of birds flew up from one of the spotlit trees.

The clouds darkened, and it started to sprinkle.

"We should be heading back," said Kurt with a frown. "We don't want to get caught in this rain…"

As they headed back down the mountain, the rain grew heavier and heavier. The dirt path became slippery, which didn't help as they began to run back toward the campsite. Ronny yelped in surprise as he slipped, landing hard on the ground. He went to push himself back up but cried out in pain the moment his hand made contact with the ground.

"Ronny?" Kurt's face was lined with worry. "What's wrong, kiddo?"

"I—I think I sprained my wrist!" he answered, afraid to move his hand at all. He held out his uninjured hand, and Kurt helped him stand up.

"Let me see your hand," said Kurt. When Ronny hesitated, Kurt smiled and said, "I won't hurt it. Trust me. I just want to look at it and make sure it's not broken. My dad's a doctor, remember?"

Reluctantly, Ronny held out his hand. He watched closely, worry lines etched into his brow, as Kurt touched his wrist in certain places. It throbbed a little, but he knew it definitely wasn't broken.

"I think you'll be okay for now," said Kurt finally, letting go of Ronny's hand. "I have some Advil back at the camp. It should hold you over until we can get to the hospital."

"H—Hospital?" said Ronny, his eyes growing wide.

"Yeah," said Kurt, confusion written on his face. "I mean, it's not broken, but you really should get it checked out."

Ronny whimpered. His wrist hurt so badly, but he always felt uncomfortable around doctors and really didn't want to go to the hospital. "I—It really doesn't hurt that badly. We don't *have* to go to the hospital...do we?"

"There's a hospital about forty-five minutes from here," said Kurt, "so we might as well go home. I'll set up the tent in my backyard, and we can camp there."

"Can...Can we go to the hospital your dad works at, then?"

"What's wrong with you?" exclaimed Kurt. "Your wrist could be very badly sprained, and you're trying to avoid going to the hospital!" He lowered his voice, not accusingly but almost as if he was ashamed he had been yelling. "You're not afraid of doctors are you?"

Ronny looked away from Kurt. "N—No, of course not. Why would I be afraid of something silly like that?"

By now, they had reached the campsite. Kurt rummaged through his bag for the bottle of Advil. He took out two and handed the pills to Ronny. "How can you be afraid of doctors when you've met my dad?"

Ronny dry-swallowed the pills, grimacing as they stuck in his throat. "I—I don't know why I'm afraid of doctors." Ronny could feel his cheeks reddening as Kurt stared at him. "I've just...always been afraid of them, and I probably always will be. It's one of those inexplicable fears people have, you know? It doesn't make any sense, but, every time I think of a doctor, I get really scared."

Silence passed between them as they stood in the shelter of the tent. Ronny could feel the rain dripping from his hair, his face, his arms... His clothes were soaked through, and he began to shiver.

After several minutes, Kurt opened up his bag and pulled out a black sweatshirt, which he handed to Ronny. "Take your shirt off and put this on instead. You'll catch a cold if you stand around soaking wet."

Ronny accepted the sweatshirt gratefully. He pulled his soaked-through shirt from his thin frame with his good hand and tossed it onto his suitcase before putting on the sweatshirt. It was a few sizes too big for him, but he sighed when he felt several degrees warmer. "Thank you," he mumbled.

Kurt pulled off his own clothes and put dry ones on. "You should put on some dry pants, too, and some dry socks."

Ronny nodded and pulled his sweatpants out of his suitcase. He felt several sizes larger than he actually was, the dry clothes practically falling off his body. He picked up his towel and used it to dry his hair.

"You have really pretty hair," said Kurt.

Ronny jumped when he realized Kurt was standing right next to him. "Oh! Th...Thanks."

"The grey highlights look really nice." Kurt leaned in even closer, his warm breath tickling Ronny's neck. "You know...I have a fear of thunder. Not even lightning, just thunder. I'm scared of something that won't even hurt me." He began to gather up loose articles of clothing and shoving them into the suitcases, not even bothering to put the clothes in the right person's bag. "Come on, we're going to the hospital. I'll be right there holding your hand. You'll be fine."

Ronny felt himself falling in love all over again.

Chapter Six

Ronny Cohen squeezed Kurt's hand as if his life depended on it. He hadn't even seen the doctor, and he was shaking like a leaf. Because Ronny's left wrist was sprained and his right hand was currently squeezing the life out of Kurt's left hand, Kurt took it upon himself to fill out the paperwork. By the time they were admitted to see the doctor, Kurt's hand probably needed just as much help as Ronny's wrist.

And yet, Kurt never said one word about the pain.

"Well, it's not broken," said the doctor after she had analyzed the X-rays, "but it is a pretty bad sprain."

"I could have told you that," muttered Kurt.

Ronny would have laughed if he hadn't been shaking so badly.

The doctor cast an exasperated look at Kurt. She knew his father and had actually been over to their house a few times for dinner; Kurt was secretly trying to hook them up. "Kurt, if you're going to be such a smart ass, I'm going to leave right now."

Kurt's expression seemed strained. "No, please, don't go." He had personally requested Dr. Yates in hopes that Ronny would relax around someone Kurt knew. In all honesty, Ronny *had* relaxed...but only a little.

Dr. Yates snickered at Kurt's expression. "Like I'd leave a cute little kid like this all alone." She ruffled Ronny's hair. "Is he your boyfriend?"

Ronny froze, but Kurt merely laughed. "Nah, he's my best friend!"

Dr. Yates winked at Ronny. "Sorry to put you on the spot like that, darling. I'm always teasing Kurt. I swear he's gay, but he's into this new theory he's created—how does it go again?"

Kurt rolled his eyes. "Rebecca here thinks I'm crazy. I believe that there's one person out there for everyone—a soul mate, if you will. If it's a girl, that's cool, but if it's a guy, that's cool, too."

"But he has a girlfriend," added Dr. Yates. "It just doesn't fit into his whole plan."

Kurt shrugged. "Well, I mean, I'm still in high school. I'm not ready to go looking for my soul mate yet. Might as well pass the time with a fine piece of ass."

Dr. Yates smacked him across the head. "I thought your plan included you to 'save yourself' for your soul mate, or whatever."

Kurt rubbed the back of his head. "Gee, Rebecca, I was just kidding. Besides, Lauren's just… Oh! Did Dad tell you? She's coming to visit in two weeks!"

Ronny had been feeing increasingly happier as the conversation had gone on. Kurt was open to liking guys! But, at the mention of Lauren, his euphoric high crashed downward. He had forgotten Lauren was coming to visit. He had forgotten that his crush was already taken…

"He didn't tell me," said Dr. Yates, "but he *did* invite me over for dinner tonight. Was this your doing, Kurt? I know about your plan to get us together."

Kurt laughed. "Actually, no, I haven't spoken to my dad about you in a few weeks. But, hey, if you still like him…"

Dr. Yates grinned. "Maybe I do, and maybe I don't." She looked at Ronny as if just remembering he was there. "Ronny, you should have spoken up. You were probably bored to tears, listening to dumb old Kurt and his love life. All right, take some more Advil in a few hours. For now, just keep ice on it and try to keep your wrist elevated. And make sure you don't use your wrist for *anything* for the next few days until it's fully healed. You should be fine by next Wednesday."

"Th—Thank you, Doctor," mumbled Ronny.

"No problem, dear." She smiled at him, and Ronny smiled weakly back. Then, the smile was gone, and she turned worriedly toward Kurt. "Is he going to be all right if I come over for dinner tonight?"

Kurt nodded. "Yeah, he's fine around my dad. You'll be fine, won't you, Ronny?"

Ronny took in a deep breath and said shakily, "Yes, I'll be fine."

Dr. Yates's smile was back in place. "All right, boys, you can go home. And I'll see you tonight around seven o'clock."

They had been in the car for nearly half an hour before Ronny had finally calmed down. "Thank you so much, Kurt… I don't know what I'd do without you."

"Probably wouldn't be spraining your wrist, is what you'd be doing," said Kurt with a laugh. "Sorry if Rebecca intimidated you. For being so slender, she sure is…big, you know? Like, if you only heard her voice, you'd imagine someone who'd fill up the room, like she's ten feet tall or something. Maybe she wasn't the best choice of doctors…"

"No, she was perfect… I really appreciate it, Kurt. Really."

"No problem. You're my best friend. You shouldn't expect any less from me."

Ronny smiled. Kurt had no idea how much of a hold he had over Ronny's heart. "So, how does Rebecca know your dad? Doesn't she live pretty far away?"

"Actually, she lives about thirty minutes from my house. It's her commute to work that's hell. She's thinking about transferring to the hospital my dad works at, seeing as how it's only about twenty minutes from her house. Oh—I'm rambling. They met at some doctor Christmas party. Her brother is really good friends with my dad. They've known each other for nearly two years now, and they haven't even realized that they both like each other. It's kind of funny, actually."

Ronny adjusted the ice on his wrist and frowned. Kurt noticed Ronny's change in expression and quickly asked what was wrong.

"It's nothing really," said Ronny.

"You know," said Kurt seriously, "whenever you say that, I can tell that something's really bothering you. Now, what is it?"

Ronny sighed, knowing he could keep nothing from Kurt. "It's just that… Well, I mean, you have Lauren, and your dad and Rebecca have each other, even if they don't know it yet. Ben came home the other day with a new girlfriend. Even Georgina's got a list of boys' numbers. You never realize how happy people are when they're in a relationship until you're the only one you know who's single."

Kurt placed his hand on Ronny's thigh and squeezed gently. "Relax, kiddo. You'll find that special girl one of these days."

Ronny almost laughed. "Yeah… Maybe."

Dinner that evening was an interesting spectacle. Peter Vaughn followed Dr. Yates around like a lost puppy the moment she walked in the door. Her wavy blonde hair fell just below her shoulders. She wore a little black dress that perfectly emphasized her hourglass figure. If she took off her high heels, the top of her head would barely reach Peter's chin.

Peter Vaughn had also dressed up for the occasion. He had even styled his hair a little, and Ronny had to admit that the usually gruff-looking man cleaned up really well.

Peter and Rebecca flirted like there was no tomorrow, causing an endless source of amusement for Ronny and Kurt. Ronny had expected Kurt to feel awkward watching his father trying to hook up with someone else, but Kurt merely egged them on. They fed off of each other's happiness, and, even though no alcohol was consumed, an outsider would have assumed they were drunker than hell.

It was past four o'clock in the morning before Ronny and Kurt went to bed. Ronny was glad the next day was a school holiday; otherwise, the two of them probably would have skipped.

"Hey, Kurt?" asked Ronny from his place on the floor.

"Hmm?"

"How come your dad chose tonight to ask Dr. Rebecca over for dinner when he knew full well we weren't going to be home?"

A knock sounded on their door. "Kurt," came Mr. Vaughn's voice. He sounded angry. He wiggled the doorknob, and Ronny was surprised to hear that it was locked. "Kurt, Rebecca can't find her car keys. Do you know what happened to them?"

Kurt tried to hold back his laugh. "No, Dad, I don't. Well, why doesn't she just stay over?"

"Kurt, I'm warning you… I'll break down this door if I have to."

"What, you don't trust your own son?"

"No." His voice softened as he said, "Hey, Ronny, have you seen Dr. Yates's car keys?"

"No, sir," Ronny answered truthfully. "I'm sorry. I haven't seen them." He looked curiously up at Kurt, who pointed silently at the car keys lying on his dresser. Ronny's eyes widened, realizing Kurt's plan.

"Well, if you see them…" The rest of Peter's sentence was drowned out by Kurt's sudden burst of laughter.

➤ ◄

The next week went by all too quickly for Ronny. The closer it came to Lauren's arrival, the more depressed he felt. Kurt, on the other hand, grew more and more excited.

"I can't wait for you to meet Lauren!" he exclaimed on Friday morning at school. "She is definitely the coolest girl I've ever met. I'm sure you'll love her!"

"Yeah," answered Ronny, his smile strained. "I'm sure I will…"

On Sunday, he drove over to Kurt's house and they waited for Lauren to arrive. When the doorbell rang, Ronny felt as if he would literally be sick. Kurt opened the door, and a girl around their age with dark brown hair threw herself into Kurt's open arms.

"Kurt!" she exclaimed. "I can't believe it's really you!" She pressed her lips against his cheek. "I've missed you *so* much!"

Kurt hugged her, having to stoop a little due to their height difference. "Lauren! I've missed you, too!"

Ronny felt miserable when he realized how cute they looked together. Lauren's light brown eyes and Kurt's blue-grey eyes were shining with pure joy. Ronny felt as if he were interrupting, and he tried to retreat to the kitchen.

"Lauren," said Kurt, grabbing onto Ronny's upper arm. "This is Ronny. You know, the one I've been telling you about?"

Lauren smiled as she shook Ronny's hand. Even her teeth were perfect, Ronny noticed, realizing that *everything* about her was perfect… "It's so great to meet you finally! You're all Kurt ever talks about."

Ronny tried to return the smile, but there was no warmth behind this gesture. She smirked, almost as if she knew exactly why Ronny was being so cold, about how jealous he was at the moment. She waited until Kurt had taken her bags into the guest room before whispering into Ronny's ear, "You're a *lot* cuter than he gives you credit."

Ronny blinked. Was she flirting with him? "Thank you," he replied tersely.

She winked, and Ronny had never felt so angry at anyone in his life. She had Kurt, which, in Ronny's opinion, was equivalent to anything anyone would ever need…yet she was flirting with him? Why would anyone be stupid enough to throw away someone as amazing as Kurt?

She noticed Ronny's anger and was confused. When Kurt came back into the room, however, she was immediately all smiles again.

Two-faced bitch.

"Do you want to go out somewhere, just the three of us?" Kurt asked.

Lauren giggled. "You make it seem like all three of us are dating," she said. Kurt blushed and she quickly said, "Why don't you two go do something? I'm pretty tired, so I'm going to take a nap. I don't want you two to be bored out of your minds just sitting around."

Kurt glanced at Ronny. "Your call, kiddo," he said. "What do you want to do?"

"I think…I'm going to go home."

"I'm sorry Ronny was so rude earlier," said Kurt once Lauren had woken up from her nap. "He's usually so nice… I don't know what came over him."

Lauren chuckled. "I know exactly what it is. I can't believe you're too dense to notice."

Kurt was confused. "Notice what?"

"No, I want you to figure it out for yourself." She motioned for Kurt to come sit next to her on the bed. "You know, he's a lot cuter than you described."

Immediately, a far-off dreamy look passed over Kurt's eyes. "I know… but how do you put something that beautiful into words? Everything about him, from the creamy white color of his skin to the yellow-green of his eyes… If you looked 'beautiful' up in the dictionary, his picture would be right there."

"*Beautiful*, noun, Ronny Cohen," said Lauren with a grin.

"Exactly!" laughed Kurt.

A sad look passed over her face for a moment before she could put her façade back in place. She straddled Kurt's legs and kissed the tip of his nose. "I came out here to tell you something. I'm leaving tomorrow morning."

Kurt's eyes widened. "What? But you just got here!"

"I know," she said. "I came out here to tell you something: I'm breaking up with you."

Kurt felt his jaw drop. "Wh—What? I mean, I know we live really far away from each other, but—"

"No, no, no, it's not that," she said with a laugh. She crawled off Kurt's lap and sat down beside him, leaning up against him. "I like you—a lot. But, I can't be with someone whose heart is with someone else."

"What are you talking about?"

She closed her eyes and pressed her lips against Kurt's: their first kiss. "Kurt, am I a mean person?"

"Lauren, what's going on? I don't understand—"

"Answer the question."

"No, you're not mean, but you sure are scaring the hell out of me!"

She moved toward the headboard and pulled her pillow to her chest, hugging it. "I can't be with someone when I know I'm taking him away from someone else. There's someone else that's deeply in love with you, you know."

Kurt tried not to blink as he stared at her, fearing he would miss a change in her expression, a clue that maybe this whole thing was one cruel joke.

Her eyes met his. "When I kissed you just now…did you feel anything?"

"What? That's not—" He paused and suddenly felt extremely guilty when he realized that his answer was "no."

She stood up. "Kurt Vaughn, you're my best friend, and nothing's going to change that. I just don't think that you're up for this relationship. It's not how far away we are—that's never bothered me—but when I look at you, and you're thinking of someone else…it hurts, you know?" She held out her hands and helped him stand up.

"So…you came all the way out here just to break up with me?"

"Oh, heavens, no! I came out here to see you! Tomorrow, I'm going to my grandmother's. She lives near here. I think I told you that…"

Kurt nodded. "Yeah, you've mentioned it."

She wrapped her arms around his waist and rested her head on his chest. "I really wanted to see you, you know… I thought that if I saw you, I would realize that you still loved me. But, after this afternoon, I realized that you've never loved me as more than a friend."

Kurt didn't know what to say. "I—I'm sorry…"

She laughed. "Don't be sorry! You remember that theory of yours, about having one soul mate out there somewhere?" She waited until he nodded before she continued. "I'm jealous of you, you know? You've already met your soul mate. I just wish I could meet mine…" She sighed. "Well, I guess there's only one thing left to do."

"What's that?"

"You get to make me a going away dinner!" She leaned up and kissed him on the chin before letting go of him and walking toward the kitchen. "I think I'd like baked salmon…with rice, maybe. Or maybe pork chops."

Kurt laughed. "You sure are a strange girl."

"Yeah… I know."

Chapter Seven

Ronny Cohen was anxious when he woke up the next morning for school. He almost convinced himself not to go to school at all, but he knew he needed to talk to Kurt. Usually one for form fitting clothes, he forewent his usual style and pulled on a pair of sweatpants and a loose T-shirt. Even though it wasn't very cold outside, he pulled a hoodie on over his shirt. He frowned when he realized it was the one he had borrowed from Kurt during their camping trip.

Georgina immediately noticed something was up. Their parents had already gone off to work and Benji was still upstairs getting ready, so they were the only two in the kitchen.

"Ronny?" she said as he sat down to eat his breakfast. "Ronny, what's wrong?"

"Nothing," he mumbled.

She stood up so she was taller than he was. She put her hands on her hips and huffed. "Ronny Cohen. I am your sister. Do not lie to me."

"What makes you think I'm lying?" Ronny asked.

"For one, you look like you stole someone else's clothes. Sweats? Honestly, that's not your style. Obviously *something's* wrong. For two, you're not even *looking* at me. For three…I heard you crying last night."

Ronny was so grateful that his sister was worried about him that he wrapped his arms around her and pulled her into a deep hug. He felt tears stinging his eyes as soon as their skin made contact.

"Now, what is it?" Georgina asked softly, returning the hug. "Is it about Kurt?"

Ronny nodded. "I met his girlfriend," he whimpered. "He's so happy with her. It…It broke my heart!"

Georgina rubbed small circles along her brother's back. "Shh… Ronny, it's all right. I know it hurts…"

Benji walked into the room and glared. "Georgina, what are you doing?"

Georgina jumped, not having heard her brother come into the room, but she didn't let go of Ronny. "Geez, Benji! You scared me!"

Ronny tried to stem the flow of tears, but every time he pictured Lauren and Kurt together, he felt his heart break a little more.

Benji fixed himself a bowl of cereal and sat down at the table. He barely glanced at Ronny before asking his sister, "What's wrong with him?"

Georgina glared at Benji. "You don't even care, do you?" she snapped before storming out of the room.

Ronny felt the absence of Georgina in his heart more than from the lack of warmth pressed against his body. His eyes were red and swollen, but at least he had stopped crying. He pretended not to notice Benji as he stared into his cereal bowl.

Benji shifted uncomfortably in his chair. Ronny looked as if he were contemplating drowning himself in his milk. He really had no idea how to handle this situation now that Georgina had left the room. Ever since he was eleven years old, when the family first found out Ronny was gay, it had been hammered into his head to treat Ronny worse than dirt. While Ronny had been away at the boarding school, Mr. and Mrs. Cohen had warned Benji not to tell any of his friends about his older brother.

Benji realized that he was just as confused about Ronny now as he had been three years ago. Ronny was his brother. Shouldn't he be supportive of him, no matter what he did? But their parents…

"Er, Ronny…" Benji had no idea what he was going to say to his brother, but the words were out of his mouth before he could stop them. Ronny looked up, taken aback that Benji had dared to speak to him. "Uh… Sorry."

Ronny wrinkled his brow in confusion. "Sorry for what?" His voice was weak and hoarse from crying.

Benji took a deep breath and decided once and for all to ignore everything his parents had ever hammered into his head. "I'm sorry, you know? It's just that…Mom and Dad, when they found you…making out with Tony Randall… I mean, you can imagine how much of a shock that would be to anyone."

Ronny felt his eyes narrow. "No, not really."

Benji's mouth suddenly felt dry under his older brother's glare…but he knew he had to continue. "Look, I know that it's probably three years too late, but I'm really trying to apologize here. I mean, after they sent you off to St. Paul's, I was practically forbidden even to think about you. I have this image of you planted in my mind of being some promiscuous whore, some superficial sinner… You've barely been home these past three years, but now that you're back for good…I've had a lot of time to think about things…"

"*Things*?" Ronny scoffed. "Like what?"

Benji sighed. "I'm about to tell you something I've never told anyone else before. It's the reason I've resented you so much, something that had nothing to do with Mom or Dad's 'love' for you."

Ronny was silent, waiting for him to continue. Benji was hoping that Ronny would have said something and shifted uncomfortably in his seat when he was met only by silence.

"Umm… Well, the night before they found you and Tony in your room… I had stumbled across some, uh, gay porn on the Internet." He turned beet red the moment the words were out of his mouth. "Before that day, the thought didn't even cross my mind that two boys could like each other, and suddenly I was knee-deep in gay men. Can you imagine how freaked out I was when the next day our parents practically disowned you for being gay? I mean…how was that supposed to make me feel, when I had just found out what gay *was*? I thought to myself, 'What if I'm gay? Will Mom and Dad disown me, too?'" He realized he didn't know where he was supposed to look, and his eyes shifted all around the kitchen.

"I know it's not much of an excuse for my having been such a jerk to you," continued Benji, "but…I really am sorry."

Ronny stared across the table at his brother. "I can't say I completely forgive you right now," he said. "It's been three really hard years for me. At the time I needed family the most…you all abandoned me."

Benji hung his head. "I didn't expect you to forgive me at all…"

Ronny smiled. "I know. But you're my brother. I'd love you no matter what you did."

At those words, Benji completely broke down.

Ronny pulled up to the school with Benji halfway through first period. They waited until the bell rang before sneaking inside, camouflaging themselves with the crowd.

During math class, they had a test, so Ronny was unable to speak to Kurt until lunch. Kurt rushed through the line to buy his lunch and quickly hurried over to the small table where he and Ronny sat every day.

"Ronny," he said the moment he had sat down, "I want to tell you—"

Ronny pressed his fingers to his lips, signaling for Kurt to be quiet. His eyes were still a little puffy, but he had finally gotten over his grief. He stared out the window for a few minutes before deciding to get it over with…to get over his crush on Kurt and let him be happy with Lauren.

"Kurt," he started slowly, casting his yellow-green eyes down at his sandwich. "I want to tell you… No, I want to apologize for how I acted yesterday. There is no excuse for how rude I was to Lauren. Can I come over later and apologize to her, too?"

Kurt shook his head. "No, she's not there… She broke up with me."

Ronny's eyes widened. "Y—You're kidding? But you two looked so happy together! Oh, Kurt, I'm so sorry!"

"Nah, don't be. I never really liked her as a girlfriend anyway. It was selfish of me to keep her tied down when she could have been looking around for other boyfriends. She's a really sweet girl, you know."

"So…did she go back to California, then?"

"No, her grandmother lives out here, so she went to stay with her for the rest of the week. We're still friends, though, which I'm glad for. I really only thought of her as a friend, anyway."

Ronny didn't know what to say. It seemed that everyone had benefited from this, even Lauren, who was now able to find a boyfriend who lived less than 1,000 miles away.

"She said something very interesting to me, though," said Kurt slowly.

"Hmm? What's that?"

"She said… She said that she knew someone who loved me, and she was taking me away from her… But, I mean, that doesn't make any sense, does it? The only friend of mine she's ever met has been you."

Ronny felt his stomach do a back flip and suddenly understood everything that had transpired between him and Lauren the previous day. She hadn't been flirting with him; she had known that he was head over heels in love with Kurt!

For the first time since he had met Kurt, he was glad that he was dumb as a brick. He had practically come right out and said "Ronny loves Kurt" and didn't even notice.

"Ah well," said Kurt, giving up on shedding some light on the "mysterious" message. "Lauren likes to talk in riddles. I can usually figure them out, but… Ah, whatever. Hey, do you still want to come over later?"

Ronny smiled. "Actually…my brother and I made up this morning. I was thinking about hanging out with him today. Sorry."

"Hey, that's great!" said Kurt. "I'm really glad you guys made up. Did you want to come over tomorrow, then?"

"Yeah, all right…"

By the last class of the day, nearly everyone in the school knew that Ronny and Benji were brothers.

"I told one person," said Benji grimly, "and two hours later, the entire school knew. You're not mad at me, are you?"

Ronny shook his head. "No, not really. I've never had so many people know my name in my entire life. It's rather amusing, really."

When the bell rang, Ronny walked out to his car and was surprised to see Benji waiting for him there. He seemed lost in his own thoughts and didn't notice Ronny until the older boy had opened the door.

"So…" Benji shifted uncomfortably in the leather seat as they drove off. "What… What do you want to do? I mean…we're not going to do anything… you know…are we?"

Ronny turned his radio up, his Umbrellas Without a Handle CD still in the player. "Benji," he said a little more forcefully than he had meant to. "Just because I'm gay doesn't mean I like to do 'gay' things. I'm a guy, just like you and all the other men in this world. I like to do 'guy' things."

"Oh…"

Ronny bit his tongue in order to stop himself from snapping at his brother. "Look, why don't we just go home? We can always hang out there, and you don't have to worry about being seen in public with me—"

"No!" said Benji quickly. "No, I *want* to spend time with you, I really do! But, it's hard! I haven't really spoken to you since before St. Paul's, and even then, we weren't really close. It was always you and Georgina… You never let me play with you."

"That's because you always cut Georgina's Barbies' hair."

Benji laughed. "Do you remember what I used to tell Mom when she would yell at me? I would tell her that I was practicing to be a barber."

Ronny relaxed a little, remembering a time when they were all happy. "I remember Mom let you get away with it that first time, and little Georgie was *so mad* at you."

"Yeah, she tried to flush my racecars down the toilet…but they got stuck, remember? And there was that huge flood—"

"All I remember was that *I* was the one who always got in trouble because of you two. While Mom was cleaning up your messes and passing out Band-Aids, Dad was always scolding me. He always told me, 'You're the oldest, Ronny. You have to look after your younger siblings.'"

"I would have sympathy for you…except that Georgie and I were always spanked, and Dad always gave you a Popsicle. Besides, you were always standing *right there* when we would fight!"

"Yeah, I remember I would stand there and say, 'You're going to get in trouble.' And then I would bring you a pair of scissors, anyway."

Ronny and Benji had been laughing so hard that they were nearly to the point of tears.

"Why don't we pull over somewhere?" Benji asked between laughs. "Hey, there's Dickson Café. Why don't we stop there and get a milkshake? I haven't been there in *ages*."

Ronny pulled into the café's small parking lot and stopped the car. Hardly anyone in their city stopped at the café, which was evident by how few cars were in the parking lot. With a quick glance at the license plates, Ronny realized that most of the cars were from people who were out of town and wanted to experience a little "local color."

Ronny and Benji stepped into the café and were immediately greeted with 70s music and the heavy smell of grease. They grinned at each other, remembering the times they had spent here as kids. Neither of their parents were very good cooks, so they had spent most of their childhood either eating frozen dinners or eating out.

The two brothers were seated in a booth by the back window. They picked up the greasy menus and scanned for things that they remembered eating as kids.

"Can you believe that I had a Star Cola Milkshake every time I was in here?" said Ronny, making a face. "It was pretty much just Coke syrup in a glass. I don't know how I could stomach that thing."

"I always asked the waitress for Cockroach Pie," said Benji. "I thought I was the funniest kid in the world." His eyes lit up. "Do you remember that time she actually brought one out for me? I was so excited, I ate that entire thing!"

Ronny smirked. "Mom told me not to tell you…but that was really Spinach Casserole."

Benji's face fell. "Oh… You know, after all these years, I've been trying to figure out what that was and why it tasted like old feet." His expression changed, and he blushed. "Er… Ronny, I wanted to ask you something…"

"Sorry," said Ronny with a smirk. "I don't know of any cute boys you can date."

Benji's mouth fell open. "What? No! It's nothing like that!" He pouted slightly. "And I was being serious, you know."

"Oh. Sorry. What is it, then?"

"I—I just wanted to know…" The color of Benji's cheeks darkened. "I wanted to know…if you and, umm…if you and Kurt are, you know…together?"

"Why?"

"Because…when you look at him or talk about him, you always look so happy. But when you're by yourself…you always look like someone just died or something. I'm…worried about you."

Ronny was sure he would have started crying had the waitress not come up to the table with their milkshakes. "You're—You're *worried* about me?" He repeated the words with such disbelief. Benji, his little brother who had treated him worse than dirt and had pretended he didn't even *exist*, was *worried* about him?

Benji bit his lip, feeling small and vulnerable with Ronny's yellow-green eyes trained on him. "Yeah, I mean…you're so depressed all the time. I can hear you crying at night sometimes. All of these neurotic feelings you have bottled up can't be good for you."

Ronny hung his head, staring at the table. "Yeah, well…it's complicated. He's always flirting with me, but that's just how he is. And I keep fooling myself into thinking that we might have a chance, but…"

"Doesn't he have a girlfriend?" Benji questioned.

"Had, actually," Ronny answered. "But…he's straight, then, right?"

Benji sipped slowly on his strawberry milkshake. He couldn't believe he giving relationship advice to his brother. "Not necessarily." he said only once the silence was too much. "He could always be bi, you know."

"Whatever he is," growled Ronny, "he should do it without being so damn fucking hot!" He angrily stuck his straw into his mouth and sipped on his vanilla milkshake.

Benji found himself laughing. When Ronny turned his anger onto his little brother, he held up his hands defensively. "No, don't look at me like that! I'm not making fun of you or anything! You just…you looked like a dog that had its toy taken away, or something! It was—" He stopped himself, not really sure what word he should use.

"It was what?" Ronny prompted with a smile.

"Uh…funny," Benji finished lamely.

"Right…" Ronny winked at his brother. "Because I'm *so* hilarious."

"Yeah, yeah, whatever…"

Chapter Eight

Ronny Cohen knew something was wrong the moment he and Benji pulled into the driveway. Georgina was sitting on the front stoop with her chin in her hands, waiting for them. Ronny could see his parents standing just inside the doorway, their bodies casting a shadow over the top of Georgina's head.

"Mom and Dad want to talk to you," said Georgina grimly to Ronny. "Benji, you need to stay out here with me...even though we'll probably be able to hear everything that's said, anyway." She shouted the last part, casting an angry glance over her shoulder toward their parents.

"Do you know what's wrong?" Benji asked, confused.

"Same thing as always, I'd expect," she answered. "You're usually not home when they yell at Ronny. You're lucky."

Ronny tensed up and walked inside. His parents professed that the only reason that they had these little "talks" was because they loved him. The moment the door closed behind him, his parents were immediately chewing off his ear.

Mrs. Cohen was the first to start. "I was using the computer, and one of Georgina's friends sent her a message asking her if you and a certain Kurt Vaughn were together. Isn't this the same Kurt Vaughn that you've been spending so much time with these past few weeks?"

"We've decided to send you back to St. Paul's," Ronald, Sr. told his son.

"You do realize," snapped Ronny, "that just because it's a Catholic school, that doesn't mean there aren't any other gays there, right? Why can't you just accept that I'm gay so I can move on with my life?"

Ronny's parents looked as if they had been slapped. For the first time, Ronny decided that it was time to stand up to his parents.

"Look, Mom, Dad. I know it has to be hard for you, seeing as how I will never give you any grandchildren or what-the-fuck-ever, but think of how hard it's been for me. You suddenly stopped loving me—"

"We never—"

Ronny held up his hand, and his mother stopped. "You suddenly stopped loving me and sent me off to a boarding school three hours away. I hated myself those first few months. I didn't understand what I had done wrong. I almost killed myself, you know. I had been abandoned by everyone I loved just because I was a little different, so what did it matter if I was alive or dead?" His anger had been rising to dangerously high levels, and he was finding it hard to keep his temper in check.

"Y—You tried to kill yourself?" Mrs. Cohen gasped, her voice hardly above a whisper.

"Yeah, I did," retorted Ronny. "I didn't think anyone in this world loved me anymore. Until I got my new roommate, Steven, who honestly didn't care if I was gay or straight, I didn't have any friends at St. Paul's. I had kept to myself mostly, afraid that no one would accept me anyway. I was sick nearly every morning when I woke up, and the teachers thought I was anorexic."

"Why didn't you tell us any of this?" Mr. Cohen demanded.

"I didn't think it was important," Ronny answered truthfully. "You had your mind set on hating me. I didn't want to bother you."

Mrs. Cohen broke down in tears. "Y—You're not a b—bother, R—Ronny. You're just… We only wanted what was best for you. It's just…when you were fourteen years old, and we found you k—kissing that…boy…we thought you were going through a phase. Just e—experimenting. But, when we realized you were serious…"

"You had already developed the habit of hating me?" Ronny finished for him acidly.

"We've never *hated* you, Ronny," sobbed Mrs. Cohen.

"Could have fooled me," he shot back. "And threatening to send me back to St. Paul's? Nice touch there."

"We just want what's best for you," Mr. Cohen said.

Benji had slammed open the front door and looked practically livid, never before having heard what his parents said directly to his older brother. "For *you*, you mean?" he spat. "You're *ashamed* of him! Ashamed of your gay son! I'll admit that I was ashamed of him, too, but that was only a reflection of *your* thoughts! I realize now that I could never again abandon my brother like that."

Ronny stood there with his mouth hanging open, taken aback Benji's force. "B—Benji, you don't have to—"

"No," cut in Benji. "No, this is something I need to do. Mom, Dad... Ronny is my brother—and your son! I've accepted him for what he is; now it's your turn."

Mr. and Mrs. Cohen stood dumbstruck. Never before had their children revolted against them like this—

Georgina came inside and joined the fray. She took Ronny's hand with her left and Benji's with her right. She didn't say anything; she merely stood there staring directly at her parents, trying her best to meet their eyes as they tried their best to avoid hers.

Ronny finally broke away and headed upstairs. Nothing had been resolved, but he did feel a little better knowing that he had his brother and sister to count on. He collapsed on his bed, pulled out his cell phone, and dialed Steven's number, desperately needing someone to talk to.

Steven began talking the moment he answered the phone. "Ronny! I was *just* about to call you! I met this girl; she's new. We're in physics together. Her name's Heather. Long brown hair, dark brown eyes, skin the color of porcelain—the whole shebang. Anyway, we went on our first date last night. It wasn't much, seeing as how we're not allowed off campus. We just walked around—"

"Steven..."

Steven immediately quit talking when he heard Ronny whisper his name. "Ronny? What's wrong?"

"We got in another fight..."

Steven growled. "Want me to come over there and bitch slap them like there's no tomorrow?"

"No..."

"They have no right to treat you like this!" he snarled. "You're a good kid, you know that right? You're my best friend! You're the nicest kid I've ever met. You don't deserve to put up with the shit they put you through."

"Benji and Georgina stood up for me, though."

Steven couldn't keep the smile out of his voice. "One small step for Ronny Cohen, one giant leap for...uh...gaykind."

"Steven… Never again."

Steven laughed. He was glad when Ronny had gotten over the whole "everyone hates me mentality" that most people at St. Paul's started out with. Poor St. Paul's. It seemed to be a magnet school for children whose parents had had enough of them. When Ronny, unlike so many others, had finally learned to trust and love again, Steven was amazed at how sweet the boy was. A lot of other students were bitter and angry at the world, but not Ronny. He was so optimistic about everything.

"Steven? Are you there?"

"What? Oh, yeah, I'm still here. You feeling any better, Ronny?"

"A little…," he answered truthfully. "I'm sorry I called and ruined your moment of happiness. I'm so excited about you and Heather."

Steven smiled. "You know… She reminds me of you. The way you both smile, no matter how hard life's getting to be… The way your eyes light up when something amuses you, no matter how small a thing it might be… If I didn't know any better, I would have sworn that you were related."

Ronny snickered. "Sounds like you're in love."

"You know what? I think I am."

"You and me both," answered Ronny.

"Well, Ronny, I'm going to go. Even you aren't worth wasting minutes on. Listen, I can't wait to see you. Are you going to come visit any time soon?"

"Yeah, I hope so."

"That's awesome! I'll see you whenever, then. Don't even call; just surprise me. Bye, Ronny!"

"Bye, Steven."

There was a knock at Ronny's door. "Come in!" he called.

His mother poked her head around the doorframe, and Ronny immediately wished he could crawl up in a corner and die. "What do you want?" he snarled.

Mrs. Cohen looked slightly taken aback but advanced anyway. Sitting at the very edge of Ronny's bed, she looked as if she wished she could be anywhere else in the world. "Ronny, I need to talk to you."

"Yeah?"

"Ronny… You have to understand something. It's not like your father and I don't love you, but…I've grown up knowing that those with homosexual tendencies will never enter the gates of Heaven. I don't want my children burning in the flames of Hell."

Ronny felt his eyes narrow, but he tried his best to keep the fury from his voice. "You hold the Bible in front of you as a shield, using it to preach your own philosophies."

"That's not—"

"I don't believe in any god that would forsake his own children." He felt his voice crack, his emotions seesawing back and forth between extreme anger and extreme sadness. "If He created me, why would he turn me from His kingdom?" His voice rose. "That's just bullshit, Mom!"

Mrs. Cohen shrugged. "I didn't make the rules. That's just how it is."

"*Mom*! Think for yourself for once! Realize how wrong that is!"

His mother looked away. "I just want what's best for my children," she all but whispered.

Ronny's anger gave way to frustration. How could she believe she was giving "what was best" for him?

"Mom," he said more calmly than before. "I can't help what I am. I can't drink some magic potion and become straight. When I realized my preference, I was ready for years of prejudice and intolerance, but—I didn't expect it from my *family*!"

After several minutes, Mrs. Cohen said softly. "I know… It's just that all these years I've been deluding myself into thinking you were just going through a phase. I didn't expect you to…stay gay."

Ronny took his mother's hands in his own. "Mom, look at me. I'm Ronny Cohen. I'm your son. I'd be the same person whether I liked guys or girls. It doesn't matter!"

His mother shook her head. "I know, I know!" She let out a dry sob that shook her whole body. "And since you've been back home…I've been trying to give it a chance. Without you here, I could—but now that you're home and I see you…I remember that you're my son. I remember those nine months I carried you before you took your first breath. And when I see you—I—I remember how you came into this world with your umbilical cord wrapped around your neck and how you almost didn't make it—"

"I—I didn't know that." Ronny's hand subconsciously went to his neck and rubbed it.

"I—I tried so hard to keep it from you because—because if I said it aloud, it would be real, and I would have to remember it again…and go through that pain again… Oh, Ronny, I don't know what I would ever do without you here in this world. I love you so much…" She took her son in her arms and smoothed his hair. "I think…maybe…I think I can finally reach acceptance." She collapsed, a weary pile of bones. "I'm so sorry," she whispered in his ear.

"It's okay, Mom." It took all of his strength to form those three simple words.

With tears pouring from her eyes and a strained smile on her lips, she said, "I suppose all we have left to do is convince your father."

"Ha! Yeah… I guess so."

Ronny's cell phone rang. His mother smiled weakly. "I'll let you get that." Once she had stood up and left the room, he answered it without even looking at the caller ID.

"Ronny!" shouted Kurt from the other end. "I'm so glad I reached you! I have the best news ever!"

Ronny was a little taken aback by Kurt's enthusiasm, which contrasted so much with his current feelings.

Kurt didn't bother to wait for Ronny to ask what his news was. He jumped right into it: "Okay, so, Dad went on a date with Rebecca tonight to some fancy restaurant. They just got back about ten minutes ago, and guess what she had on her finger! *An engagement ring*! I'm so happy for them!"

"Wow! That's great!"

Ronny could hear Kurt's dad and Rebecca laughing and shouting in the background, and he felt a small pang of jealousy. He could remember when his parents had been that happy, but…that was a long time ago…

Kurt was talking again. "We're having the engagement party this Saturday. They invited all their doctor friends, so I would love it if you came and kept me company. Well, I mean, I'd want you there anyway…but even more so so that I'll have someone to talk to."

"All right. I'll be there."

"You will? Awesome! You're the best, Ronny!"

Ronny sighed when Kurt hung up the phone. He fell back against his bed, and before he knew it, he had fallen fast asleep.

Ronny woke up groggy on Saturday morning. It had rained all day Friday, and it was still drizzling the next morning. The rain seriously affected his mood, and he was quite grumpy when he headed downstairs for breakfast. The sun did not peek out from behind the clouds until nearly sunset, right as Ronny was leaving his house to go to Kurt's for the engagement party.

Even though Ronny had already congratulated both Rebecca and Peter Vaughn, he found himself shaking their hands once more. "Congratulations, Mr. Vaughn and the future Mrs. Vaughn."

Kurt pulled Ronny away from the suffocating crowd and into the kitchen. "What did I tell you? Those doctors…they're too smart for their own good! Here, help me make dinner. Will you pass me the salt?"

Ronny and Kurt remained in the kitchen for the first half of the party. They were so busy making dinner that they barely had time to think or breathe, much less socialize.

"Hey, Ronny," said Kurt while they were cleaning up the kitchen. "You good in here? I need to run to the restroom. I had about five or six glasses of that fruit punch. It was *so* good!"

Ronny snickered. "All right, yeah, sure, Kurt. You'd just better not be bailing on me," he called as Kurt rushed out of the room.

Rebecca staggered into the room, a glass of fruit punch in her hand. "Hey, Ronny," she said a tad loudly, her words a little slurred. "You didn't drink any of the fruit punch, did you?"

"No, why?"

"Ted just"—hic!—"Ted just told us that he, uh, he"—hic!—"put some rum into the fruit punch." She smiled. "I was just making sure you didn't have any. You're"—hic!—"underage, and you have to"—hic!—"drive home tonight!"

Ronny paled and nearly dropped the dish he was holding. When Kurt sauntered into the kitchen a few minutes later, he was carrying a half empty glass of fruit punch. Ronny snatched the glass away from him and tossed the contents down the drain.

"Hey… I was drinking that!"

Ronny wondered how Kurt was able to drink so much liquor and still manage to be standing up straight. "Don't drink anymore!" Ronny scolded. "Apparently someone spiked the punch!"

"Oh…" He scratched his chin thoughtfully. "You know…I *thought* that it tasted a little strange. Thought it was just me, though." Even though he wasn't even moving, he stumbled and nearly fell over. He grabbed onto a chair to hold himself up. "Uh oh… Somebody get a technician out here and get this world to stop spinning."

"Maybe you should sit down," suggested Ronny.

Peter Vaughn sprinted into the kitchen, his face a little red from the liquor. "Hey! You guys should come into the other room! We're playing Twister!"

Ronny shook his head slightly. Middle aged doctors playing a children's game? What was this world coming to?

He put away the last dish and looked behind him where he had last seen Kurt…only to find the room empty. He headed into the living room and saw Kurt tangled up amidst the other doctors.

"Right foot, yellow!" someone called.

Six different people went to move at the same time, and, partially because of their intoxication and partially because of the difficulty of the game, collapsed a pile of giggles and limbs. Ronny rolled his eyes when he noticed Kurt at the bottom of the pile.

Rebecca stumbled over to Ronny and swung her arm around his shoulders. "Ronny!" Her usually loud voice was amplified by the spiked punch. "Ronny, I'm so glad you could make it to my engagement party!" She was overtaken by a fit of giggles and was unable to continue.

"Rebecca's such a lightweight," said the infamous punch spiker, Ted, with a large grin on his face. Ronny noticed, with amusement, that he and Ted were the only two who were sober.

"RONNY!" came Kurt's booming voice from across the room. "Ronny! Come play Twister with us!"

"No," said Ronny flatly.

Three minutes later, he tried to forget how his right foot had gotten on blue, his left hand on green, his right hand and left foot on red, and his body pressed up against Kurt's. The brunette had literally dragged Ronny onto the playing mat. It also didn't help that Rebecca seemed determined that everyone at their little party was having "fun." She stood there with her hands on her hips, glaring every time Ronny would grumble and complain about having to play.

"Right foot, red."

Ronny's eyes squeezed shut as he slowly drew his right root over to join his other foot and his right hand. He felt someone knock into his left foot, and because his right foot was in the air, he fell to the ground. He landed on top of someone, and he was already muttering apologies before he opened his eyes…and found himself staring right into Kurt's face.

"Hello, Ronny," said Kurt, slightly amused. "I seem to have fallen over."

Ronny could smell the sweet scent of fruit punch on his breath. He tried to move and get off Kurt, but someone had fallen on top of him. Because of the high levels of intoxication, it seemed to take hours for everyone to disentangle themselves.

"H—Hi, Kurt," said Ronny, blushing slightly as he realized how close their lips were. He was pressed right up against Kurt, and he could practically feel the muscles through his shirt.

"You're really very pretty, you know?"

Ronny could feel his face turn bright red. "Thank you, Kurt."

Blame it on the alcohol, blame it on the alcohol! I will not *allow myself to fall any deeper in love with Kurt!*

Kurt buried his nose in Ronny's hair. "And you smell really good, too. Just like peaches—with a tiny bit of cinnamon."

"K—Kurt?"

"What? It's a nice combination." He wriggled his hand out from underneath someone else's body and ran it through Ronny's hair. "Your hair is so soft, too. You're like a little puppy."

Ronny realized that he and Kurt were the only ones left on the floor and the others had gotten up. He quickly rolled off the brunette and tried to hide his blush.

Kurt sat up and looked at Ronny curiously. "You sure are red. Are you hot or something? I'll get Dad to turn on the air conditioner." He went to stand up, but lost his balance and tumbled forward onto Ronny. "Stop moving around!" said Kurt a little crossly.

Ronny had leaned backward in order to avoid smacking his chin against Kurt's head, and now they were both lying on the floor, Kurt's head resting against Ronny's chest.

Peter Vaughn came over and helped the two boys stand up. "Maybe you should go to bed, Kurt," he suggested. He helped Ronny bring the boy into his room before rejoining his fiancée and the other guests.

"Ronny," said Kurt, lying on his bed staring up at his ceiling blankly. "Have you ever been in love?"

Ronny sat down on the edge of the bed. "Why?"

Kurt shrugged. "No reason. Just wondering."

A small smile passed across his lips. "Yeah, I've been in love before. I'm in love with someone right now."

"Really?" asked Kurt, sitting up in bed, his eyes shining brightly. "With whom?"

Ronny stuck out his tongue playfully and said, "Not telling."

Kurt lay back down on the bed. "Oh. Well, I guess that's okay. I wasn't going to tell you who I'm in love with, either." He paused before asking, "So, how's your anarchy theory coming along?"

"I…" He trailed off. "I want to tell you, Kurt, I really do! But…I still don't think I'm ready quite yet."

"Does it have anything to do with your shark's tooth necklace?"

Ronny reached up and fingered the charm. "I guess you could say that," he said softly. "Steven gave it to me after I told him about…that thing. He said that he didn't care what I thought and that we were still best friends." He smiled. "He was right, you know. He didn't care. And he didn't look at me any differently. But I was so scared when I told him, you know? And I'm even more scared to tell you…because I don't want you to leave me. I'm sick of being alone."

Kurt sat back up and wrapped his arms around Ronny. "I won't leave you. Ever. Even if you get sick of me and hate me, I'm never leaving you alone."

"Thank you, Kurt." He laughed when he realized that Kurt had fallen into a deep sleep with his head resting on Ronny's shoulder. "I love you," he whispered. He laid Kurt down gently onto the bed before falling asleep beside him.

Chapter Nine

RONNY COHEN WOKE up and realized what he had to do. He had to tell Kurt that he was gay and that he was deeply in love with him. All of this hiding behind a smoke screen was really taking a toll on his sanity. If he didn't tell him soon, he felt like a dam of emotions would burst and he would end up doing something stupid—like letting Kurt slip through his fingers forever.

It was now or never.

But that didn't mean that he could tell him in person, face to face.

Kurt Vaughn woke up with a nasty headache. He was going to *kill* Ted for spiking the punch and not telling him! Otherwise he would have just drunk water or something. He rolled over and noticed that Ronny's smiling face wasn't there to greet him. Instead, his father was standing over him with a note in his hand.

"Ronny left this on the kitchen table for you this morning, Kurt," said Peter Vaughn.

Kurt took the note from his father a little tentatively. What would have made Ronny run out on them without saying goodbye?

Dear Kurt, Sorry I left without saying good bye. But, in my defense, it's already nine o'clock, and you're still sound asleep. There's something I need to tell you, but I'm too shy to tell you face-to-face. So, please call me when you wake up. I really need to tell you this and get it off my chest. Talk to you later, Ronny.

Kurt glanced up at his father, a confused expression on his face. "What—?"

"He seemed really nervous about something," said his father with a shrug. "Rebecca said she knew what was going on, but I couldn't get anything out of her before she left. She kept prattling on and on about 'woman's intuition' or some shit like that."

"Right…"

Kurt waited until his father walked out of the room before picking up his cell phone and calling Ronny. "Hey, Ronny, I got your note. What's up?"

Ronny could feel his stomach twisting in a knot. He couldn't believe that he was about to come out to his best friend. Being a natural introvert, he was finding it more and more difficult to come up with the right words with each passing second. A wave of nausea passed over him, and he almost hung up the phone.

"Ronny, you there, kiddo?"

"Y—Yeah," Ronny answered shakily. He took a deep breath and said, "Kurt, I want to tell you about…about my anarchy."

Kurt was silent. He certainly hadn't been expecting this. In all honesty, he had been hoping Ronny could have told him in person. It felt almost impersonal for them to do this over the phone, but…if this was the only way Ronny felt comfortable doing it, then he was fine with that.

"Go ahead," Kurt prompted. "I'm listening."

"I…I'm not like other boys," started Ronny lamely. "I…don't really like girls like most guys do. I could never think of a girl as more than a friend."

"What are you trying to say?" Kurt knew exactly what Ronny was saying, but he wanted to hear it directly from the blond's lips.

"Kurt." Ronny was glad to hear that his voice was a lot stronger than before. "Kurt, I'm gay."

He couldn't stop the tears falling down his face when he realized that the line had gone dead.

Kurt did not come to school the next day. Or the next. Or the next.

≫ ≪

Kurt stared at his cell phone, absolutely mortified. His battery had just died at the most crucial turning point of their friendship.

"Shitshitshitshitshit!" Kurt chanted as he ran out of his room to get his house phone. He tried to block out the thoughts bombarding him, horrified at what Ronny was thinking right now. Ronny probably thought that Kurt had hung up on him on purpose, and he desperately needed to correct this assumption.

He skidded into this kitchen, his socks causing him to slide on the linoleum floor. His eyes widened in shock when he saw his father on the phone. "Dad!" he shouted. "Emergency! I need the phone—NOW!"

Peter Vaughn held his finger to his lips. Into the phone, he said, "Yes, Deborah, of course we can come up today. I'll see you in a few hours, then. Bye, Debbie."

"Aunt Deborah?" Kurt asked curiously as his father hung up the phone. "What does *she* want?"

Deborah was Kurt's mother's sister. Aunt Deborah had spent most of her life trying to make Kurt and his father feel guilty for the ex-Mrs. Courtney Vaughn walking out on them. She only called to nag.

"Uncle Frankie just died," said Peter Vaughn sadly. "The funeral is on Tuesday. Grab some clothes and get in the car. We need to leave within thirty minutes."

Kurt's jaw dropped. Uncle Frankie was Deborah's husband, and he had spent every minute of his life trying to make up for Debbie's mistakes. When Courtney had walked out on the family, Frankie was there almost every day to baby-sit Kurt, never complaining once.

Kurt would have felt horrible if he didn't go to Uncle Frankie's funeral, but…he *really* needed to call Ronny back. Besides, Uncle Frankie and Aunt Deborah lived twelve hours away.

After Peter Vaughn had gone back to his room to pack, Kurt grabbed the telephone and went to call Ronny's cell phone number. He wasn't even halfway through dialing when the battery died.

"Fuckfuckfuckfuckfuck!"

Kurt ran into his father's room. "Dad! I need your cell phone—NOW!"

"Calm down!" Peter Vaughn snapped. "Your Uncle Frankie just died! What the *hell* do you need a phone so badly for? You should be worried about *packing* instead of *socializing*! Your friends will be here when you get back. Frankie will never be here again!"

"No, no, no, it's not that!" said Kurt, holding up his hands defensively. "Besides, if I don't call Ronny back *right now*, he might not be here when I get back!"

"What are you talking about?" Peter Vaughn looked really surprised. "Of course he'll be here. You guys are best friends, right?"

"Cell phone," said Kurt weakly. "Please…"

Peter Vaughn reached into his pocket and fished around for his phone. Confused, he checked under his bed…on his nightstand…in his jacket pocket… "Sorry, Kurt, I don't know where it is. Why don't you use another phone?"

"My cell battery is dead, and so is the house phone's battery!"

"And so is Uncle Frankie. Now, go pack!"

Kurt hung his head. He trudged into his room looking like a kicked puppy. He tried to find his charger as he packed, but it was nowhere to be found. He took out his suitcase, threw some clothes in it, and put it into his dad's car. They left within fifteen minutes.

It was nearly three o'clock in the morning by the time Kurt and his father reached his aunt's house. Kurt had fallen asleep on the ride over, and his dad carried him into the house. When Kurt awoke the next morning, the house was alive with noise. It seemed everyone and their cousin had stayed the night in Deborah's tiny house. He finally managed to nab a quick shower before getting dressed. His shirt wasn't even all the way over his head before his father had pushed him outside and into the car.

Halfway to his grandmother's house, Kurt realized he still hadn't called Ronny. He looked around the car, praying his father's phone was somewhere in the car but was sadly mistaken. After visiting his grandmother for a bit, he tried to grab a chance to call Ronny on her house phone. Halfway through dialing the number, however, his Aunt Deborah snatched the phone from his hands.

"Leave the line open!" she hissed. "We're waiting for a call from the funeral home!"

"Can I use your cell phone, then?" Kurt asked pleadingly, ready to get down on his knees and beg if he had to.

"No," she snapped. "And if I see you on the phone, I'll—"

"That's *enough*, Deborah," a woman snapped.

Kurt froze and felt the blood drain from his face. Even though Uncle Frankie had been her brother-in-law, he hadn't, even for a moment, considered the fact that…*she* would be there.

He turned around and came face-to-face with a handsome woman. She had dark skin, almost the exact same shade as Kurt's, and dark brown hair with blue-grey eyes. Her jaw was tense and there was no shine to her eyes.

"Hello, mother." Kurt hoped that she didn't pick up on the undercurrent of bitter animosity his voice held, but from the look in her eyes, he was sure she did.

"Hello, Kurt," she said. Her voice was a little deep, and the sugar coat she usually added was missing. "I'm glad you came. For a while, I didn't think you would."

"We loved Uncle Frankie," said Peter Vaughn tersely, coming up behind Kurt. He put his right hand on his son's shoulder, almost as if he were protecting the boy. "We wouldn't miss his funeral for the world. He was all we had after you walked out on us."

Kurt wasn't sure if her eyes really narrowed with intense dislike, or if it was his own twisted image of her that produced an inaccuracy.

"It's nice to see you here, Peter." Her blood-red lips curled back in a semblance of a snarl. "After all these years, it's nice to know that nothing about you has changed. Always having to play the part of a hero, pretending that you love my family and shit."

"Courtney." Mrs. Tatum, Kurt's grandmother, had crept silently up behind them, making no more noise than a cat, a miraculous feat for a woman in her late 70s. "Courtney, why don't you go help Deborah in the kitchen? I don't want you and your ex-husband getting in a fight at an already upsetting event."

"Yes, Mother," she snapped. "Whatever you say." She purposely walked in the opposite direction of the kitchen. A few seconds later, they heard the front door slam.

"I'm sorry, Mrs. Tatum," said Peter sincerely. "I didn't think she would try to cause a scene."

"I know, dear." Mrs. Tatum sighed. "Why don't you come into the kitchen, and I'll make you some tea?"

"Thank you. You've always been so nice…"

Kurt waited a few minutes, making sure no one was paying attention to him, before snatching up the phone. Just as he was about to start dialing, however, it rang in his hands. "Damn it!" he hissed. He followed his grandmother into the kitchen and handed her the phone. Deciding to wait for her to get off the phone, he sat with her in the kitchen and listened as she made the arrangements for the funeral.

Three hours later, Kurt still hadn't had a chance to use a phone. Every time someone would hang up, the phone would ring again. When he finally had his chance to use it…the battery died.

"ARGH! DOES ANYONE HAVE A CELL PHONE I CAN BORROW?"

Immediately, his aunt was upon him. "You're supposed to be in mourning," she hissed. "Stop trying to socialize."

"I *am* mourning!" Kurt said through gritted teeth. "I'm mourning the fact that I'm about to lose the best thing that's ever happened to me."

They went out to dinner that night, and Kurt was immersed in family members that he didn't even know he had. He never did see his mother again, and he was unable to get access to a telephone, even for a few seconds.

He was exhausted by the time he made it back to his aunt's house. Having found his charger, he went to plug in his cell phone, but he couldn't find it. Absolutely furious, he lay down in bed, cursing everything he could think of. He didn't realize how tired he was and fell asleep within minutes.

The funeral was hell. His mother showed up close to the end, drunk, and tried to pick a fight with her ex-husband. Eventually, the cops came and took her away. The whole scene left a bad taste in everyone's mouths, and Kurt was angry that his final image of his uncle had been tarnished.

They stayed out the rest of the day. Kurt was finally able to borrow a cell phone from his Great Uncle Albert and was livid when he realized that he didn't have any service.

Kurt woke his father up at six o'clock in the morning and dragged him out to the car, which already had their suitcases in it. He hopped in the driver's seat and didn't even wait for his father to finish buckling his seat belt before speeding away.

"Calm down, Kurt!" said Peter Vaughn, his face white as a sheet as they took a sharp turn at over 50 miles an hour. "I know you're mad at your mother for ruining the funeral, but—"

"Don't talk to me," snarled Kurt. "We have to get home. I *have* to talk to Ronny!"

"What is all of this about?" Peter snapped, hoping against all hope that they wouldn't get pulled over…or kill anyone. "Ever since we left, you've been trying to get a hold of Ronny. Why is this so important?"

Kurt glanced over at his father. "I—I love him, Dad. I really love him. I have to tell him that."

Peter Vaughn smiled. "Rebecca will be so happy to know that. She's been wondering how long it would take you to figure it out. She knew you loved him the moment you two stepped foot into the hospital the day Ronny sprained his wrist."

≫ ≪

Ronny Cohen was miserable. He hadn't wanted to go to school that morning, and he sure as hell didn't want to stay the extra two hours after school doing research in the library.

Kurt had spent so much of his time saying that he wouldn't act any differently around him once he knew all about Ronny. Besides, just because he was gay didn't mean that he had to act so *dramatically*! Skipping school for three days? Honestly!

Tears blurred his vision as he made his way home. He swore he would never speak to Kurt again, but his heart told him otherwise. He pulled into his driveway and was surprised to see a figure hunched over on his front stoop. The figure looked up, and Ronny was furious when he realized it was Kurt. He turned off his engine and threw his car door open.

If he had stopped to notice how miserable Kurt looked, he wouldn't have slapped him so hard across the face.

"Where the *fuck* have you been?" Ronny yelled.

Kurt, who had never heard Ronny yell and had therefore never been on the receiving end of his anger, stood staring in shock at the usually quiet and calm boy. "Ronny, I—"

Ronny cut him off angrily. "No, forget it. And, you know what? Forget *you*! Here I was thinking that you were Mr. Amazing with your 'oh, I won't change my opinion of you!' And then I tell you I'm gay, and you avoid me for three days! How is that supposed to make me feel? So, I don't want any of your excuses, you—you—you—!"

"Ronny…" Kurt's plea was so low that had Ronny not seen his lips move, he wouldn't have known that he had spoken at all. And then he noticed. Kurt's head hung down in shame, tears dripping from his eyes. He looked absolutely crestfallen. "Ronny…" He took a step forward and wrapped his arms around the blond. "I'm so sorry…"

Despite his better judgment, Ronny returned the hug. "Where have you been?"

"My cell phone battery died," said Kurt softly.

"Well, why didn't you just charge it?"

"I went to grab my house phone, but my dad was talking to my Aunt Deborah. My Uncle Frankie died, and I had to go to his funeral. Trust me, every second of each day I was trying to find a phone to call you, but somehow, I couldn't ever get to one."

"For three whole days?"

Kurt's arms tightened around Ronny. "I think someone somewhere was trying to get me to tell you this in person: Ronny Cohen, I love you."

Ronny froze, thinking that he had misheard Kurt. "Please don't joke around with me, Kurt. You've already broken my heart once this week."

"I'm not joking," said Kurt seriously. He pulled away from Ronny so he could look him in the eyes. "I swear I'm not. You have no idea how freaked out I was, not being able to get a hold of you all that time."

"Kurt…"

Ronny was on the verge of saying, "I love you, too" when Kurt pressed his lips lightly against Ronny's. The kiss deepened as Kurt pulled Ronny impossibly closer to his body.

They pulled apart after what seemed like decades, each immeasurably happy.

"I'll never leave you, Ronny Cohen. I told you this before. Now do you believe me?"

Ronny smirked. "Not sure. I think I might need a little more convincing."

Epilogue

Ronny Cohen had never been so happy in his life.

He reached out and held Kurt's hand as they stood at the altar, watching as Mr. Peter Vaughn and Ms. Rebecca Yates became husband and wife. Ronny watched with a happy heart and an impossibly large grin on his face. He was a little surprised when Kurt turned around with tears in his eyes.

"I can't believe they're almost married!" he whispered. He began dancing a little, unable to contain his excitement.

The ceremony ended, and if Ronny hadn't been holding onto his hand, Kurt would have rushed forward to pull his dad into a bone-crushing hug. Kurt's cheers blended into the crowd's but practically deafened the blond.

"I'm so happy for him!" Kurt cried. "I've never seen him this happy with any woman, not since before Mom walked out on us, anyway. He's never been good with women since then, hasn't trusted them much—"

Kurt didn't close his mouth until they had reached the reception, chatting on and on about how Rebecca was the perfect woman for his father. Ronny had heard these speeches from Kurt hundreds of times in the days preceding the wedding, but they still hadn't lost any of their charm or meaning.

Ronny squeezed Kurt's hand tighter and said, "Kurt, you are so adorable. Don't ever change."

Kurt planted a light kiss on Ronny's cheek before running off. "I have to congratulate my dad!" he shouted over his shoulder.

Ronny watched him go with a rather bemused expression. He had thought that Kurt would feel pressured to hide his relationship with Ronny from the intolerant eyes of the public, but he couldn't have been further from the truth. Kurt was more than happy to hold Ronny's hand or give unexpected kisses or vows of love.

Presently, Kurt ran back to Ronny's side with two sodas in hand. "Rebecca said that if you don't come over to see her soon, she'll go against her code as a doctor and hurt you." He grabbed Ronny's wrist and pulled him over to Rebecca's outstretched arms.

"Ronny!" she cried, planting a large, wet kiss on his cheek.

Ronny hugged her back. "Congratulations, Mrs. Vaughn. You'd better be a good mother to my boyfriend, you know."

Before she could answer, Kurt grabbed Ronny and dragged him off again. In all honesty, Ronny had thought that maybe by dating him, Kurt would become a little calmer—but it turned out quite the opposite. There seemed to be too much love in Kurt's heart for him to contain, and he was prone to several "explosions" from time to time.

"FOOD!"

Ronny felt his arm being pulled from its socket as Kurt took off toward the table. He grabbed a plate and began piling everything onto it.

"Kurt, calm down, please," said Ronny, panting a little and massaging his sore shoulder.

But Kurt was already seated at a table. Sighing, Ronny made his own plate of food before making his way over to the brunette.

"Aren't you just so happy?" Kurt asked around a mouthful of food. "Oh, you should try this quiche! Dad wanted to hire a caterer, but I snuck in some of my own dishes as well. Here…" He stuck his fork into the quiche and held it up expectantly.

The moment it touched his tongue, Ronny's taste buds erupted in satisfaction. "Mmm… Kurt, this is amazing! Your food gets better and better every time I eat it! You can come cook for me any day!"

"I suppose I can manage that…"

Ronny took a sip of his soda to hide his grin from Kurt.

His mind wandered as Kurt practically inhaled his food. He thought about his life before he found out he was gay, when his family had been extremely close. He thought about his life after he came out, when all his parents did was bitch and complain and his sister who had always loved him but was afraid and his brother who finally accepted him. He thought about his life at St. Paul's and when he first met Steven, who was the only one who accepted him for who he was.

He thought about his father, who still refused to accept his gay son, albeit he had been gradually getting a little more tolerant these past few months. Even though his mother still disagreed with his sexual preference, she kept these thoughts to herself, and Ronny knew that late at night, she was coaxing his father to do the same. While he knew he would never see eye to eye with his parents, they at least got along much better, which was more than he had ever hoped for.

He thought about when he first met Kurt…and how he had immediately fallen head-over-heels in love.

"What are you thinking about?" Kurt asked, snapping Ronny out of his trance.

"You," he answered with a grin, "and how absolutely perfect you are."

Kurt grabbed Ronny by the hand and led him out of the reception hall. For the first time since Ronny had met him, Kurt blushed and fidgeted uncomfortably. He reached into his pocket and fiddled with something nervously. "Ronny." His voice squeaked. He cleared his throat and tried again. "Ronny… You know I love you, right?"

Ronny blanched. What was Kurt talking about? Did he really feel that uncomfortable being seen with him in public? "Kurt… You're not—breaking up with me, are you?" These past six months had been utter heaven, and he couldn't imagine a life without Kurt. He felt hot tears well up in his eyes.

Immediately, Kurt's arms were wrapped tightly around the blond. "Don't ever think for even a *moment* that I would *ever* break up with you, love." He held Ronny out at arm's distance and looked him square in the eye before announcing, "Ronny Cohen, you are the best thing that's ever happened to me. I will never let you go."

"Then what—?"

Kurt held one long, slender finger to Ronny's lips. "Shh…" He replaced his finger with his lips. He pulled a small box out of his pocket, and the blush was back at full blast. "I…uh, I got this for you, Ronny."

Ronny took the small box and opened it. Inside was a little plastic ring that would probably barely fit over his pinky. "Er…thanks. Did you, uh, get this out of a quarter machine?"

"Well, no… When I was seven years old, I found this ring in a Cracker Jack box. I swore to myself that I would give it to the first person I fell in love with." He shifted uncomfortably. "I know it's really lame and all, but—"

A grin broke across Ronny's face, and he pulled the brunette into a deep kiss. "Kurt Vaughn, you are the most adorable person I've ever met in my life…and I love you for it."

"I love you, too, Ronny Cohen."